D1715809

"A great man is a child that followed his dreams."

One

The End - *Logan*

Present, 3:23 a.m.

I wake up from a slap in the face.

My father is yelling and shaking me vigorously, yet, only his rough hand hitting my face wakes me up. While my eyelids are fighting the rheum, keeping my eyes shut, I try to get out of my precious bed, and I start coughing. Suddenly I am gasping for air. I can taste smoke, and I feel the carbon dioxide trying to shut my body down. Is the house on fire? Perhaps that's why I couldn't wake up. I could've been unconscious.

In the midst of the chaos, my mother is downstairs, grabbing my five-year-old little brother and my nine-year-old sister. "Hurry up Jako!, the house is going to collapse." The desperate voice of my mother travels through the smoke upstairs.

My dad cranes his neck and yells while holding me. "If you have the kids, go! We'll be right behind you."

My dad and I make our way through my bedroom door and attempt to cross the hallway to get to the stairs. Fire is already consuming the house, and the only way out is in the hallway, which is already scorched by the flames. Time is running out, but my dad is good at acting under pressure.

Fear wells up inside me.

My dad grabs my shoulder so abruptly that I almost have whiplash. "Logan, the window, it's our only choice. We are going to get out there and jump to the tree right in front of the house, alright? We can climb down from there. You can do it!"

I look into my father's eyes, and in that second, I see all his love, worry, sadness, and many more emotions fusing into one. The family is in danger, and he is in protective mode.

I nod.

I am overwhelmed with fear, but with all the faith instilled by my mother and courage from my father, I run to the window, and he opens it as fast as he can. I stumble through it, turn around, and help him. He holds my hand as we walk quickly but carefully to the edge of the roof. We look around, and I notice, for the first time, that we are not the only ones in trouble. The neighboring houses are a conflagration. It is chaos. People are screaming; I see many on fire, running, and others already on the ground unrecognizable from all the deep burns. I am terrified, but I don't want to let my father see that.

At the edge of the roof, we search for a way to escape the burning house. Already safe, my mother and two little siblings spot us and watching with fear, my little sister Minda yells, "dad, brother, be careful!"

My little brother grabs my mother's legs and refuses to watch us jump to the tree. My mother hugs my brother to comfort him.

I take a few steps back, run, and jump to the tree that seems a mile away, knowing that it is only a few feet from me. My heart is beating hard as I hear the frame of the roof cracking under the intense heat; I feel my blood rushing through my veins, adrenaline at its purest. I reach the tree and crash into a branch. Unfortunately, it can't hold my weight and snaps. My eyes widen, my muscles clench, and my body prepares for the inevitable fall.

My family watches me fall and screams my name, "LOGAN!"

I hit the ground, and pain shoots through my back with throbbing so intense my ancestors must have felt it. Fortunately, I can still move, so I don't think I broke anything. My little siblings run and help me get up.

"Are you ok, big brother?" Luke asks.

"Yes, 'little hulk,'" I said while getting up and moaning with pain.

My father asks from the edge of the roof, "Logan, are you alright?"

"Yes, father. Hurry up and get down here, the house won't hold much longer."

My father jumps to the tree while I limp off most of my pain. He is more clever than I am and has no problem climbing down safely. He runs over to us. "Do not worry, I promise I'll protect you from whatever is happening," he tells us. "I won't let any of you get hurt by anybody, and everything is going to be ok."

We all look at each other and hug for a few seconds.

My parents' cars are burning. We have to walk or run from whatever is going on.

"Let's go, too much going on here. We are going to find a safe place to figure out what to do," my dad says. Then he looks at me, puts his hand on my shoulders, and continues, "*Hijo*, I know you are only sixteen years old, but today is the day you become a man and show what you are made of. You and I will keep your mother and siblings safe. I have faith in you, and I know you are ready to step up if something happens to me. You will keep this family safe."

I am proud and excited when my father trusts me. He is my hero, even if he doesn't know it.

"Yes, Sir!" I reply.

"Ok, Logan you will be in the back, I will be leading the formation. Belisa, you will be right in front of Logan and the two little ones between us. Come on, let's go!"

We start running, and the noise is unbearable as people wail; gas stations are exploding, cars crashing, it feels like the world is ending. We are oblivious to what the hell is happening. All we know is that we have to move away.

Twenty minutes of walking, and running and my little brother complains, "daddy, daddy! Can we stop for a second? I'm tired and thirsty."

My dad knows we must keep going to find answers and get away from the presumed danger, so he turns around and says to Luke, "we need to keep moving, ok? I am going to put you on my shoulders and keep walking." He grabs Luke from under his arms and lifts him on his shoulders.

After a couple of miles, we see Jacob's bar on the corner of Dragon Street and Sixteenth Avenue. The windows had shattered from some force inside, littering the street with glass. Blood is splattered everywhere and, strangely, it is the only building not damaged by flames. It's as if something came out of the place.

Upon entering the bar, we see a TV on the wall. My mother says, "let's see if it works, we could watch the news or something. We need to know what is going on."

The TV is damaged, and my father knows it is likely not working, but he humors us and checks it anyway.

"Yes, Belisa, let me try and see if it works," my father says.

The TV turns on, and all we can see and hear is static. Our faces turn sullen. We face each other and sigh. We sit down for now. It is far quieter in this part of the city. My dad is thinking about what we should do next. My mom is consoling my little siblings, and I am guarding the door. I don't know why I am defending it, but something feels out of place. *Is this a war?* Everything feels strange.

After a few minutes of thinking, my dad gets up, puts his hands on his waist, and says, "we don't have any information on what is going on. The city has been burned, destroyed by something, and we have no place to stay. We could have been bombed, but I don't know how the government could have missed something on this scale. People are dying, and others are injured trying to escape this hell. We need to know what is going on so we can have a plan of action. We're gonna go to the news station that's about three miles away."

"We have no other options but to try," my mother agrees, and we are on the move.

That bar though, it made me wonder. Nothing about it looked normal. *What the hell is going on?*

As we walk with renewed purpose to the news station, we glance at buildings collapsing in flames and ash. Some structures seem bent at odd angles. The city doesn't look like bombs did this to it.

I am thirsty, we all are, and every place that could have water is ruined. Luke and Minda have not complained at all; they are reticent, which is unusual for those little, energetic kids. We trust my dad; he is our superhero. He has always been there for us, for me, even though we don't share the same blood; he would give his life for me, I think.

9

About fifteen minutes into the walk, we hear a girl's voice calling for help. It sounds as if she is in pain and crying. "Help, please, somebody help!' The pleading doesn't stop and gets louder as we walk.

My family starts looking around, and my dad yells back, "where are you? Keep yelling so we can find you and help!"

Suddenly, a girl around my age appears out of a dark alley by the Kamikaze dancing club.

As she walks towards us, I see her clothing, arms, face, and legs are smeared with blood. My mother looks at her, astonished, grabs her softly from the shoulders, and asks, "oh my God! ... what happened? Are you hurt?"

The girl seems out of it. Her face reflects fear, her body is trembling, and she does not say a word. She might be in shock and hadn't even noticed she was yelling. My dad is patient, but we need to know if she knows something. He insists with a reassuring voice, "Hey, I know this must be hard for you, it's obvious that something terrible happened to you. I can see that. But we need to know if you know something about what it is going on. We will protect you until we can find your family, I promise. But to do that, we need to know what is going on."

The girl looks at my dad in the eyes; her posture changes. She is not shaking anymore. "You cannot protect me or yourselves...no-one can. They are too strong to be stopped. Their abilities are not of this world."

"What? Who did you see? Please tell us; we need to know. We will believe you," my mother says.

"Ma'am, it doesn't matter if you believe me or not. It is only a matter of time before they get everybody."

My dad sighs and asks her name.

"My name is Liath; you can call me Li for short."

"Well, my name is Jako; this is my wife, Belisa. My two little kids are Luke and Minda and my son, Logan. We're gonna stick together, so if you can tell us more, then please do. For now, we are on our way to the news station."

"No, no, you cannot go down there! They also came out from there. We will be killed, and everything is destroyed. I was there."

"What do we do then? Who are these people, and why would another country do this?" My dad asks.

"You should just hide," Liath replies.

Little Luke is quivering and grabs mom firmly, putting his head against her thigh and closing his eyes. "Mom, I don't want you to die; let's hide."

My mother gives Luke a comforting smile and tells him, "don't worry, son, we won't let anybody hurt you. We will defend each other from whatever comes. We will survive this, ok? Do not be scared."

Luke looks up with tears running down his cheeks and says, "okay, mom." She kneels and kisses him on the forehead.

11

I walk towards my dad, and when we are face to face, I whisper, "Dad, we need to keep moving. We can ask questions later. We are in the middle of the street, and I don't think it's a good idea if this is a terrorist attack. If what Liath said is true, they're hunting us. We need to find a building where we can think calmly and try to convince her to tell us what she saw."

"You are completely right, son." He then directs his words to everybody. "We need to move. Let's go, everyone, the same formation as we started. Liath will be in front of you, Logan. Let's move!"

Although it feels like days have passed since the incident, it has been only a couple of hours. The sun now begins to rise.

Our life was beautiful. We never suffered or worried about anything, ever. We had everything we could have asked for. Perhaps, that's why this madness is happening.

We choose a direction and walk.

Two

The Lost Girl - *Jako*

My family. I have to protect my family.

My wife is a strong woman. She has been with me for a long time, even when I went through a phase of confusion. I didn't know what I wanted, I was lost for a while, and she stuck with me. She has shown unconditional support in everything I do. Even though, sometimes, when we have our quarrels, she brings up my decision to join the armed forces without consulting her first. We went through tough times, but we are still together and stronger than ever. Now, I'll bet she is glad I had decided to join the service and rose through the ranks.

My excellence in the field had landed me within the Special Forces Unit, known as Jaguar Knights. Not the usual branch you hear about, but it has prepared me for everything I had always hoped never to encounter.

In this situation, I need those skills acquired from my training; I won't let them down. I will

13

protect them, all of them, even the girl, Li. I hope she decides to tell us what she saw and what happened to her, but she is still acting strange.

This attack is most likely a riot, but whatever she saw traumatized her. I am worried, but I need to keep my composure, so my family does not panic. I love them so much that I'd give my life for them.

6:42 a.m.

The dense smoke coming from the houses, buildings, cars, and everything else that was destroyed creates a smog, limiting visibility while at the same time, making us nauseous. Three hours have passed, walking down the broken streets of my home, and besides Liath, we haven't seen anyone else alive. Our only company is charred bodies and others who seem to have suffered more gruesome deaths at the hands of… something. Terrorists couldn't tear people apart. Aside from the flames, none of the deaths seem natural. I see no bullets, hear no aircraft. Maybe Liath is not delusional. I must keep myself alert.

We continue walking, Minda is awfully quiet. She is never this quiet, but the situation could've affected her more than I thought, so I stop and ask, "Minda, how are you doing? Are you ok? You are very quiet."

She hangs her head.

"Come on; you know you can tell me anything."

Minda looks up. "Yes, daddy, I am fine. I am just thinking of all these people who died, and I hope they passed peacefully. There must be a reason for this to happen."

This touches me. My daughter, being nine years old, worries more about the souls of those who already have died than her own. I smile tenderly and say in words my wife would use, "sweetie, God will hear your prayers, he listens and works according to his best judgment. Sometimes we don't understand what he does, but for everything, there is a reason greater than us." Minda smiles and nods.

I smile back, stand up, and sigh. "Let's keep moving."

I cannot make sense of why we haven't seen anyone else alive, which is extremely strange. Perhaps people are just hiding, as Liath suggested. However, I can't worry about that for now, I know we need food and water before anything else. My kids and wife need strength to keep going and remain focused.

Everything is a wreck, every single building. Everywhere we look is destroyed and deserted. Where did everybody go for God's sake? I really don't know what to do. But how can I tell this to my wife?

But wait, the military base has plenty of Meals Ready to Eat (MREs) and weapons in the cages down in the basement. Hopefully, the flames didn't penetrate there as well.

I stop.

Belisa shoots me a concerned look. "What is wrong? Did you see something?

"Nothing happened B, I just thought of something. We could go to the military base and search for food and weapons so we can at least have a chance to defend ourselves. They have dozens of boxes of MREs in the basement to feed soldiers when they have drills, and M4 assault rifles and semi-automatic handguns to train. That place might not be completely wiped out."

"Really, daddy? Do you think we could find food there?" Minda says.

I take a knee and say, "yes, kiddo, let's go and look!"

I stand up and grab my wife's hands and nod my head to reassure her that we would get through this.

We arrive at the base safely, but the others are starting to show signs of sore feet and blisters. I don't know how long we've been walking.

The massive complex is marred from the outside, but otherwise unharmed. If this was a military action, wouldn't they have targeted the base instead of civilians? The perimeter of the facility is protected by an electric fence. *How can we get in there?*

I get close to the fence and looking farther down the line; I spot a hole. I walk closer and inspect. It seems as if something chewed, bent, and clawed its way out. The opening was at least seven feet high, with remnants of skin and dried blood caught on the damaged links.

My heart pounds.

The skin is not entirely human; it seems thicker and discolored.

"Dad, is it a good idea to walk in there?" Logan asks.

I look at him and look back at the hole.

My wife has doubts as well, and she expresses herself. "Jako, let me talk with you for a minute?" She turns around and tells Logan to watch the kids.

She takes me a few feet away, keeping our children on her sight. She seems to be putting her thoughts in order, for a few seconds and explains her theory, "Jako, this place reminded me of the bar we were in hours ago. Something came out of there; it was obvious. Something is destroying the city and that something came out of here as well."

"I was hoping you and the kids hadn't noticed, I am sorry. But you are right; this is not the riot I thought it was at the beginning. What is attacking our city is not human. The skin left hanging on the fence is something I have never seen."

Belisa replies, "not human? Do you mean… like a wild animal?"

I shake my head. "No."

"Do you mean… some kind of government experiment?" Belisa covers her mouth with her hand.

"Maybe. I have no idea. Maybe we're being invaded by aliens?"

"That is crazy! God created only us in this Universe. Maybe it is just a wild animal, something we have not seen. You watch too much 'Ancient Aliens' documentaries, Jako. Perhaps, God sent these creatures for our final judgment. Maybe, this is the end, Jako. The Bible talks about this."

I respect my wife's views and beliefs. But my beliefs differ significantly from her own. However, I've never had a decent argument for this, much less in this situation. Could this be Judgement Day? It sure seems like the end of something.

I reiterate carefully, avoiding the topic, "Belisa, I am sorry again for not telling you what was going through my head after seeing that bar. Whatever these things are, I will make sure nothing happens to our family... and that young girl."

Belisa looks at me with tenderness. "Don't be sorry for trying to keep us safe. The kids are stronger than we realized. If you think it is worth the risk to go in there and look for food, I'll support you, and we'll be right behind you."

It is time to make a decision, a decision that would affect many lives. I am used to this since I have lead groups of soldiers through dangerous situations with success, but never my own family. I cared for the men and women in my units, but my family is not trained for this kind of danger. All they have is their primal instinct to survive. The life of my family is on the line. If we don't go in there, we will be starving, yet if we go, we could encounter whatever it is that came out. But those things look like they escaped; I do not think they are there anymore.

"We are going in there, all together information. Nobody will wander around; we will stick together. We are gonna be quick. Each of us will take a box of MREs, except Luke and Minda. We will do this fast. Understood?" I instruct.

My family answers, "yes, sir!"

Liath remains quiet.

We form-up in the same order. Logan in the back, then Liath, Belisa, Minda, Luke, and I am in the front. We start walking and enter through the tear made in the fence. On the way to the main entrance of the base, we see a couple of soldiers burned and slashed, as if knives were passed through their chests. They seemed to have fought back since they still had their XM4 laser-based weapons clutched in their hands. I am not sure if the old school M4s would do any good if these XM4s hadn't even protected them.

Lab experiments? Demons?

We arrive at the main entrance only to find it replaced by rubble. Our fear increases, but we have to continue past the crumbling concrete until we reach the next building. Inside, we see walls damaged, lights hanging from the ceilings, and plumbing fixtures exposed as if a tornado blew through this place. The kids look scared, and Liath is looking around like everything is normal. I start to pay attention to her actions, and everything else

19

she does. She keeps me wary for reasons I can't explain.

As we walk further inside, a strange environmental phenomenon causes goosebumps on my skin. Down the hallway, we find the Drill Hall, and in the middle of the floor, there is a crater, seemingly the result of a blast like a bomb had imploded. I am so perplexed.

My wife asks, "what the hell is that, Jako? We need to hurry up; I don't like this. I have a bad feeling about this."

I don't reply; I barely hear her. I am looking and trying to figure out the source of the crater. I feel strange pulsing as I draw nearer, the hair on my arms and neck stands on end.

Her voice is just background noise until she goes full drill sergeant on me, "JAKO! WE HAVE TO GO; LET'S GET WHAT WE NEED AND GO!"

I snap out of it, turn around, and notice our group is too small. "Belisa, where is Luke? I ask my wife, worried, and angry at the same time. "Where is our little son?" as I finish that sentence, I feel building energy like the calm before a lightning strike. Electricity and beams of a strange light start to flare intermittently in the middle of the crater. We are looking right at them, but they seem like they are not fully there. The rays hitting the walls and floor are beginning to make a sound like if you were to tear the air as if it were paper. I feel a *pull*. It becomes loud, so loud that I can barely hear my family, who is a few steps away from me. Our hair starts to spike. Panicked, I hear from the other side of the hallway, "RUN!" It is Liath. She and Luke are holding hands.

She yells again, "FOLLOW ME; THEY ARE COMING!"

I don't think twice. I grab Belisa and Minda and yell to Logan, "COME ON!" We run towards Liath. Everything starts to shake, but not as an earthquake; it is different. The walls begin to move and crack, but the floor is unaffected. I can feel the force trying to pull me towards the crater, but it is not so strong.

Liath is running away like she's familiar with the building. We just follow her, now is not the time. Down the hallway, she turns left. As we get closer to her, I feel a slight *push* and all the trembling stops.

Liath steps into one of the soldiers' lockers attached to the wall and whispers, "shh, they are here. We must hide. There might be five of them. Last time they came in a group of five. Get in the lockers and be quiet. Hurry!"

There is no time; I can hear strange noises getting closer. I am terrified, but I won't show it. My kids need their father to be reliable. "Minda, Luke, everything will be ok. We are gonna hide and wait for whatever is out there to leave the building, okay?" I can hear the sound of footsteps, like a large animal walking on two feet.

"Hurry!" I quickly help the kids get into the lockers. Belisa and Logan squeeze into their own lockers right in front of mine. I can barely fit, but I succeed; This is the first time in my life that I've cursed my muscles. We remain quiet.

The footsteps grow softer. They must have taken a right from the hallway. A few seconds later, it is quiet again. I put my head near the door and push it out to make an opening and check the hall. It is empty.

That strange feeling on my skin remains. My mouth is dry.

In a whisper, I call everybody to come out, and for now, I don't want to question Liath. But the interrogation is long overdue. My focus is on getting supplies and getting as far away from this base as possible.

Something came into our world from somewhere else. I can feel this. That wasn't so much a door as it was a tear. Monsters have forced their way here from another dimension, world, time; I don't know. I would be intrigued by any other circumstance, but I am not about to find out right here.

Three

Queen of Klith - *Belisa*

7:30 a.m.

Yesterday, at three in the morning, Jako's alarm went off.

Jako has been out of the military for almost ten years, but his discipline has never changed. He has always been a hard worker and an early riser, always trying to make more with his life.

Every morning I received a kiss, a hug, and an "*I love you.*" Then he would get up to get ready to go to the gym and, after that, head to work.

He has never asked me to get up to cook for him. He prepares his breakfast and meals for the day. I feel blessed I found this man, or that he found me, same difference. He loves our children and me.

My days were busy, but straightforward. Very hectic in the mornings. I didn't have to do much for Jako. However, I had to do everything for my kids.

Two hours after my husband would rise from bed, my alarm would go off. I hit the snooze button. The alarm would go off again, and I would hit the snooze button again, "*five more minutes,*" I would tell myself. Sleep and I are on much better terms than it is with Jako.

When my body finally decides to listen to my mind, I would move to the left edge of the bed, sit up, and put my bare feet on the warm wood floor.

I would stand up and make my way to the bathroom.

I often washed my face and looked in the mirror and wonder how Jako could wake up so early every day to go to the gym, then work, and still come home to continue working on his personal goals; and be able to spend quality time with the kids and myself.

I am not like him. I am the polar opposite of who he is, and maybe that is why we are perfect for each other. We have the right balance.

When the clock announces six-twenty, and if I didn't hear the kids get up, I am the human alarm clock. They have to be at school at seven, and they needed to be up already, except for Luke.

I hurry to their rooms, and Logan is always snoring like a bear. "Logan, Logan...LOGAN! GET UP! you are going to be late for school!" I would have to yell, so he wakes up. He is such a deep sleeper. It could be a damn tornado, and he would not hear the destruction going on around him. The next one to be awakened would be Minda. She is a nice girl, always helping me in the house when there are chores to do. When I cook, she would run and ask if she could help. I would go to her room, down the hall from Logan's room, open the door, and walked towards her bed furtively so she could not hear me. I jumped on her bed and started playfully shaking her. "Minda! Minda! come on; it is time for school!" I said. She wakes up smiling and shaking me back and said, "you are so mean, mom!" We would laugh, then a few seconds later, I'd tell her to get you ready for school. "Go take a shower while I cook something for you and your brothers." This was a typical morning routine, and I love it.

But today, Jako's distress woke me up. It was not a kiss or a tender hug. It was him yelling and shaking me. Now our city is in danger, and we are running for our lives from creatures appearing inside of a military base. We don't know our enemy or where it comes from, but I am sure Liath knows more than she is saying. I know my husband is more worried about getting us to a safe place and finding food and water rather than questioning this girl. But she took my child, and for a second, I fear for his life. My kids are my world. I am a humanitarian, but she scares me. I understand why she did it, but I need answers now…we all do. So, I speak up, "Liath, you took my son and, even though I know why you did, for a few moments, I thought he was gone…" I start walking towards her. "…Listen to me, we need to know what you know, what you saw, and where is your family? Why are you covered with blood? Tell us!"

Liath remains quiet.

25

"Liath, I am talking to you, answer me." I am starting to get upset.

Jako steps in. "Belisa, calm down. She is just a kid. I know we are all scared, but we need to protect each other, including her."

"Don't you see, she knows something. She is hiding information that could help us survive whatever this is." I am so upset and filled with stress that tears start to form.

"I am sorry, but this is not the way. Liath will tell us what she knows when she is ready."

I don't trust that girl, but I trust my husband. I know he knows what he is doing. I hug him while tears run down my cheeks—tears for being afraid more than anything.

We keep quiet for a few moments, and Liath starts to talk, "I am neither from this world nor from this time. I am the queen of the planet, "Klith." Our world is perishing, slowly consumed by a star. My generation is the last that will see our home. Our sun is depleted of hydrogen, getting hotter and expanding, causing temperatures to rise on the planet. There is no time left. Eventually, it will be engulfed by the extreme heat; destruction is upon us. We foresaw this scenario, and we ignored it. Our scientists miscalculated the life expectancy of our system, and we began searching our universe for other suns with hospitable planets. But we soon realized that our entire universe is dying. The greatest minds of our world collaborated and created a device to manipulate the space-time continuum and were able to pinpoint a time in which our universe was once young and flourishing. We eventually found this ocean planet full of life and sent a group of Klithans to recon and to see if it was a suitable place for us to live. Earth was the third world we found, and my husband and I thought it was perfect.

We have the ability to meld our body structures into most desired species or forms. The idea was to adapt to human civilization, but there were disagreements."

Liath looks at us with pity.

"What kind of disagreements? Who disagreed?" I continue to question.

"King Lioneth, my husband, and I argued that the best way to survive was to appear like you and live within your societal norms since it is your world, and we had to respect that. But the supreme commander of our army, General Danteloth, thought differently."

"We have to move, everyone. We need to go! We are at ground zero, where these aliens cross. She can tell us more when we are completely safe. We need to get out of here," Jako says.

Logan looks at me. "Yes, mom, we should listen to my father."

Liath's story scares me, but Jako and Logan are not as baffled as I am about her story. Granted, we had witnessed unbelievable things today already. I want to know more, although my beliefs are challenged by her story. *Aren't we the only creations in this universe? Are these Angels or Demons?*

The atmosphere changes among us. Liath is not a lost, weak teenage girl. She is the queen of a planet from another time or dimension. Luke and Minda stare at her while we walk. I pull them aside. "Hey, you two, stop staring! Didn't we teach you better than that?"

Ashamed, they reply in unison, "yes, mom, we are sorry."

We keep walking, and finally, we get to the room where they store the rations and weapons.

"Come on, everyone! Grab a box. Logan and I will grab two boxes and an M4 in the event that we cannot find more in a few days," Jako says.

"That will not do you any good," Liath says.

"I know these weapons might be obsolete for your kind, but they will at least slow them down."

"You are wrong. You will be just as well off without them. Our skin cannot be penetrated easily. However, I have something you might be interested in."

"An advantage? Jako responds.

"As you mentioned a few moments ago, we have to move away from here. More Klithans will come through the wormhole." Liath begins walking away.

"Wait!" Jako says, and we follow her.

We carefully make our way back through the base and start walking away from the city towards the beautiful forest near the outskirts, being more aware of our surroundings. Thankfully, nature is untouched by the flames so far. I know that Jako doesn't really know what to do, and he won't admit it. He is a manly man and a retired Special Forces soldier. His pride is immense.

Far enough away from the military base to feel safe, Jako stops and turns around. "How long ago did your people arrive to gather information about us, Liath?"

"We sent a soldier only a few days ago in your time. He concluded that your race was very young, weak, underdeveloped, and we could colonize your world easily with minimal resistance. This report initiated an argument between the commander and me on which course of action to take."

Jako's eyebrows rise. "What do you mean, underdeveloped?"

Logan intercedes, "Father, I have read a few studies and watched science documentaries claiming that average humans can only access a small percentage of our brain potential at a time, and more than ninety percent of our DNA code is still too complex to decipher. Scientist calls it 'DNA junk.' However, many believe that if we can tap more brainpower, we'd have the ability to manipulate our bodies to a molecular level. Likely, how the Klithans are able to shapeshift."

"Really?" Jako asks and turns his attention to Liath. "Is that true? We humans could be able to shape-shift?"

Liath responds, "I am not certain about that power, specifically. Evolution is slow, but eventually, your race will evolve to be smarter, stronger, and have different abilities than we do. I have the power to manipulate genes to trigger evolution immediately for beings who possess a mind and body interconnection far above the average."

I intervene, "Jako, you don't know if this girl is telling the truth. What if she is just trying to manipulate you, or... I don't know, turn you into a slave or something? We don't know anything about anything right now."

Jako is reluctant as well. I can see it drawn in his face. But he always wanted to possess more power. After all, he is a protector. "Belisa, look at her. She is not lying. You know how I can see into someone's eyes and determine if a person is being honest or not?"

"Yes, but she is not a human being." I point at Liath, keeping my eyesight directed at Jako. "She might not express herself as we humans do. We don't know if they have developed other kinds of emotions. Or how good of an actress she is."

"Belisa, I know you could also tell that people in her race are strong. You saw the fence at the military base and all the dead bodies when coming this way. If she wanted to make me a slave, or all of us for that matter, she'd have done so a long time ago. Or she could have simply killed us. I know she is trying to help, and I need that kind of power even to stand a chance."

I remain quiet.

I wish I would just wake up and realized this is nothing more than a nightmare.

Jako turns his head to Liath. "If I do this, would there be any changes to me physically?"

"I am not certain of the type of changes that could morph your body. I am only opening your genetics to their potential. However, what is undeniable is that you will have abilities and strength hitherto undreamt of by your kind. The limitations depend on your genetics."

Jako crosses his arms and looks at the kids and me. He relaxes and begins to talk, "Belisa, I need to do this to help save our home. If I change, it will only be physically. I'll be the same Jako you love. I cannot afford to lose you and our kids because of my lack of strength. You know I would do anything to protect you. You saw what those creatures could do, and, as of right now, I am not strong enough."

This man has done nothing but works to provide for us. He has always given his all in everything that he does. I have always trusted him, and I can't stop supporting him now that he needs me the most. Tenderly, I put my hand on his cheek. "I love you. We will always be with you. You're right. We need to fight back, and she is giving us an opportunity to do so even if I am afraid and don't trust her. I trust you, and I understand this might be the only way to fight back and survive." I assure him with a more resolute look as he walks towards Liath.

Jako stands before her and cracks his neck. "I'm ready. What do I do now?"

"Close your eyes and focus. Connect the mind and body. Unify them." Liath puts her right hand on top of Jako's head. With her thumb resting on his forehead, they both close their eyes.

A sphere of bluish light begins to form around them. They levitate a foot above the ground as if the laws of physics have stopped. After a moment, the sphere of energy intensifies with an intermittent glow now visible around it. His clothes are blowing violently like a tornado is inside with them, yet the outside is calm. Jako's muscles appear to clench, and he begins yelling like he is in pain as his body contorts. Liath tries to motivate Jako; I hear them as if they are a great distance away. "Focus! The pain you are experiencing is normal and will subside." Jako gets himself under control with visible difficulty. He takes deep breaths through whatever he feels; his skin looks like shiny rubber now. I am terrified of seeing him like this.

"We are almost to the point where your body will take hold of the changes. You have immense potential, something I have never seen. Never would I have thought that humans would become something like this; your transformation will be impressive. You are not a normal human, are you? Your DNA is peculiar..." Liath muses to herself.

Jako's body further transforms. His muscles grow. Striations are visible under his skin before it becomes dense, like the bark of a great oak. His shirt tears, his blue jeans stretch, his eyes, and his hair are white. He looks so different, like a warrior from another place.

Liath slowly takes her hand off Jako's forehead. They remain floating, but the sphere of energy that surrounded them has been absorbed into him. Jako

32

looks into Liath's eyes and smiles as they begin to descend. Jako looks astonished, yet admires his new physique and strength that he now must possess from Liath. Excitement radiates from his face.

He looks like a Demigod with his big muscles and white hair. He is so tall! The sclera of his eyes, now dominant, glow brightly as his pupils have vanished. There is also a white aura radiating from him. It is astounding.

Luke and Minda are frightened by their dad's new form.

Luke grabs my leg. "Mom, is that still my daddy?"

"Yes, Luke, it is. Look at him. He is like a superhero from your comic books."

Jako approaches us, saying, "Luke, Minda, don't be afraid. It is still me. I just got stronger and possibly smarter…" Jako chuckles. "…Maybe, if I get the hang of this transformation, I'll be able to transform to my original body."

— "I am sorry, but I think it does not work like that. Your body structure is unlike ours, and through my power, your body is improved. It will not want to return to a weaker state. You will look like this until you die. This is the new you."

Jako turns to Liath. "Maybe you don't know everything. You have unlocked my potential, right? If I focus enough and train, I am sure I could change my appearance at will." Jako then gestures to Liath furtively in an effort to calm the kids down. Liath understands.

Four

The Argument - Liath

Klith:- A few days before Earth's Invasion.

Everything has a beginning and an end. It is simple science to understand that a star has a limited life span. When hydrogen and gas levels deplete the temperature rises. This event heats the surrounding planets. The star expands and becomes a red giant, and they are eventually devoured. Klith, our home, is the 4th planet from the sun and has begun to succumb to the intense heat and plasma flares.

But we are a warrior race, proud and strong. We do not give in as quickly as planets and stars.

We managed to live under the surface for a long time. Our advanced technology and our resilience gave us ways to survive. However, a new solution must be reached.

The time had come. My race would become extinct if we failed to act quickly. Even with our technologies, we cannot escape the power of nature.

Our only option was to flee and look for another planet. We could not find another hospitable planet in my universe. Our scientists and our brightest minds came together and created a plan for what they called the Galatia Miracle, a looking glass device that allowed us to search for a planet that was appropriate for us. To look for refuge in places other than space and time we were in. After a time, the device was finally built utilizing our full understanding of quantum physics, and we found a blue plant. A planet of oceans. A world with billions of living organisms. We were excited.

Over our first nutrient intake of that day, my husband and I were discussing what the course of action would be if we found a planet when our security detail came. "Excuse me, my queen. Commander Danteloth is outside with some urgent news."

"Urgent news, then why isn't he in front of us himself?" I replied.

The security detail was nervous, but she knew that the situation was…delicate.

"I am sorry, my queen. I will let him in."

I looked away unimpressed.

The doors opened, and commander Danteloth walked in hastily. "My queen, we have found what we have been looking for. A planet for our race to survive. It is a planet that was formed when the universe was eight billion years old. It is located in a medium-sized galaxy with a young star. I think we should send one of our soldiers to perform reconnaissance and report back on the various species who reside there so that we may strategize our next move. We need to move quickly. We lack the luxury of time."

I became excited about such great news. I had dared to hope but feared the worst for so long. I ran to my husband and embraced him. "My love, we can save our children, our family, and our people."

He smiled and said, "yes, Li. We need to share the great news with everyone."

I agreed and turned to Danteloth. "Commander, I will authorize you to assign your most qualified soldier to gather intel. Order him to shape-shift to the appearance of the inhabitants of the blue planet."

Commander Danteloth lifted his chest and said, "yes, ma'am."

My husband and I prepared ourselves to announce the news to the survivors who took refuge underground. Our children, Glorith and Garreth, were there looking proud. We have holographic technology to project our image to every corner of our world. But now, because of a reduction in population and our underground residence, it is used on a much smaller scale. We stood there, and the hologram projection began.

I took a deep breath. "My people, our patience and determination to find a planet to save our kind has been rewarded. Commander Danteloth came to us this morning with great news; we have discovered a world from ancient times. This planet that we now called 'Planet Blue' until we figure out its native name is a young planet we could adapt to.

36

In a few hours, we will prepare a well-trained soldier to stealthily gather information about the species living there so that we may decide our next move. We recommend that you prepare for a trip through time and space. We will keep you informed about the progress of the situation. For now, be patient and look forward to knowing that we will survive."

The crowd could be heard to the stars; the euphoria of my people was tangible. They were happy; they had Hope. I walked towards Lioneth and our children, we embraced. We were worried, but we knew we could make it. We had to.

Later that evening, when Lioneth and I prepared for sleeping hours, we discussed the events and implications of that day. We always shared our thoughts on situations to determine the best solution.

Lioneth turned on his side to lay his hands around my abdomen and said, "Liath, I am concerned about the way Danteloth handles things... he tends to be chaotic. I am almost certain he will want to approach this mission violently, no matter what we may discover from this planet."

I turned to face him, his hands still around my waist. "I know his tendencies. However, you and I will oppose it if he mentions hurting any species from that planet. We will be sure to convince everyone that we can integrate into another race's society peacefully. Both races could help each other."

"Yes, we will, my love. Let's sleep now; tomorrow could be a long day." He kissed me on the forehead.

I turned around and, still thinking about the situation, fell asleep.

Our home, the palace we lived in before we retreated below the surface, was ideally located where the light of *Klatath, our Sun,* would wake us. We had a beautiful view, breathtaking mountains that scraped the clouds. Now we had a wall of crudely cut stone for a view. It was melancholic.

I was always the first one out of bed. I let Lioneth sleep a little longer while I took a shower before I woke him. While the water flowed over me, I sighed and thought about what was coming and what we would do about moving to Planet Blue. Coming out of the shower, I saw Lioneth staring at me. His eyes, looking at me like the first time he ever saw me. We felt love, and our eyes always gave it away. As I approached to kiss him and say good morning, we heard a knock on the door that interrupted me, centimeters from his lips.

"Who is it?" I asked.

"Ma'am, Commander Lioneth is here with news about the planet we will conquer."

Conquer? Why would she say that? Unless commander Danteloth mentioned that. I hustled and got dressed to talk to Danteloth. As I was getting dressed, I told Lioneth to hurry, take a shower, and get ready.

For this day, I chose red and black attire to project power, confidence, and make it clear who was in charge of the decisions being made. I stormed to the conference room with such anger of hearing the word 'conquer.' When I opened the doors, the commander was already there, on the other side of the room, with his back facing the door. I found that very disrespectful. As he turned to me, I said, "Commander, you should be outside the door waiting for my arrival. This is my room, and I expect respect from you."

The commander looked directly at me, and after an insolent smile, said, "I am sorry, my queen. We have known each other for so long I thought of you as a family and did not think this would bother you. I ask for forgiveness and assure you it won't happen again."

Lioneth was right; the commander could not be trusted with this endeavor. His attitude could be fatal for both races. I asked the commander to take a seat to discuss the intel he gathered about the planet.

"My queen, the planet, is called Earth. It has around seven billion relatively intelligent and sentient beings, all of the same race. However, they are so primitive that they have been killing each other throughout their entire existence. War is what furthers their technology and what they turn to by default. Their technology and evolution as a species are hampered by their beliefs in a supreme being. A supreme being, also believed to be compassionate, provides comfort in their times of sorrow. They believe in eternal life through this being. I am sure that if we arrive, they will believe we are trying to invade them. They are capable of space exploration and are also looking for another suitable planet.

However, their technology limits their exploration. I believe we should take our chance, arrive by surprise, and conquer the planet. If not, many of our people could die attempting to reason with them."

The commander thought I was so naïve that I would just accept his plan, trusting his word. I could hear the inflection in his voice, the eagerness to attack and take Earth by force. If I did not act, he would take action. He was not a Klithan to reason with. As I was about to answer, my husband entered the room, and I explained the situation. Lioneth was not surprised by Danteloth's assumptions. We were quiet for a few moments. After, I turned to the commander and told him to wait outside so I could share a word with the king. He left with a slight grimace, barely imperceptible.

As soon as Danteloth closed the doors, I said to my husband, "Lioneth, you were completely right. He wants to conquer Planet Blue. We cannot allow this."

Lioneth looked annoyed. He did not want an invasion either, and he knew that Danteloth might have already made a move. "Liath, stay here! I will have words with him and make it clear that we do not desire war. If he has already made a move, he will regret it." Lioneth looked very upset. It is the first time he showed such anger.

I followed him to the door. He turned and signaled me with a gaze to stay.

"I am the Queen of this planet; I will not stay back in a time like this. This is my argument more than it is your own," I said.

He remained quiet, turned around, and kept walking until he reached the doors and opened them. "Danteloth, as the king of this planet, and therefore your king, I forbid you to make any move against any living species on Planet Blue. Queen Liath has already stated this. However, we know your history and It is…-"

Before he could finish, there was a sound and a smoldering hole where my husband's left eye used to be.

Time stopped for me at that moment. My heart skipped a beat, and one part of me died when I saw one of Danteloth's minions suddenly raise his weapon and fire a beam of superheated light. My blood went cold. My skin was frozen. Everything seemed to be passing in slow motion. "LIONETH!" I yelled as if that would bring him back. "No. No, no!" I kept yelling. I ran to him, kneeled while crying, and lifted his head. I looked toward Danteloth with tears in my eyes, with anger, disgust, and an insatiable desire to kill. He looked back with an evil smile. He did what he had wanted for years.

"Oh, my queen, now I am your king. Now we do what I say because the majority of our people are military, and my forces agree with me. We do not need to kneel to savages; we will keep our lifestyle and make those earthlings our servants. At the end of the day, they are to us as lesser species are to them."

"You bast –"

"Silent, my queen, you have said enough. We know that you disagree with us, and so do your children. I will not tolerate this. I will lock you in a cell and perhaps also kill them, in case they attempt something rash…unless you change your mind and help us take over Earth. Although I know you never will. Your lack of loyalty vilifies you in the eyes of your people."

Now, I am here on Earth, being persecuted by an evil despot. I am not sure what happened to my children, and that is killing me inside little by little.

Five

Coup - Danteloth

Present, Planet Klith.

My planet is on the brink of extinction. My people are at the crossroads of survival and destruction, and the Queen wants to negotiate? An agreement with the Earthlings for resettlement would never work in our favor. The history of Earth has shown time and time again that their species is far from their potential because they love war, violence, cruelty; They crave it, it's their instinct. It is hardwired in their brains, and they have rapidly populated the planet only to section off pieces of it to wage war continually over those borders. The only way to save our species is to invade quickly. We are more durable, faster, and more intelligent. We possess technology that they are hundreds of years away from understanding. They live by rules of physics and mathematics, and we have already bent the universe to our will. Only the death of a star could have threatened us.

As of now, I am King Danteloth, the ruler of the Klith. My entire army supports me. I have enough followers to force the council to do what I want them to do. Those who oppose me will be punished. We will conquer Earth, bring the earthlings to their knees, and make their world our own. This is not anarchy, rather, a necessary revolution led by myself, for our greater good.

Queen's Liath forced impeachment is a necessary evil. I have put Queen Liath away since she does not want to cooperate with our main concern...survival. She does not have our people's best interests in mind. Perhaps I should kill her just in case she tries something against us, but for now, I will just leave her alone.

My daughter, Aliza, 23 years old, supports my actions and is the next in command after myself. In case something happens, I trust she will fight for our cause. When Aliza turned five, I began to train her day-after-day. I made her a warrior so that she could defend herself against any enemy. Now her skills will be used for fighting against earthlings. As a father, I knew the danger my daughter would go through. However, this is only a means to an end. The cause is greater than us, and although I love my daughter, I need her to do as much as she is able to save our people.

As the new ruler of this world, I have to give my speech. I make my way to the conference room and turn on the projection holograms. "For those of you who do not know me, let me introduce myself. I am Commander Danteloth, leader of the military that defends our planet. That being said, I have to confess that I have done unforgivable things. However, it was a necessary evil. My predecessors were naïve and indecisive about the actions needed for our survival. They were more concerned about the well-being of Planet Blue's residents than for our people. We have no time; we must act. We don't need a meticulous plan; we need only to move fast and conquer!" I pause as I hear scattered but plenty of applause. The planet is not divided equally, but there are those who oppose me.

"I know that it is not simple to accept the way I have done things. The king is dead, and the queen is locked away" I can hear the crowd murmuring amongst each other. "I am sorry for those of you that supported our previous leaders, but they lacked the qualities needed for our species survival in times like these. Trust me; I have your best interests in mind. Klithans, I am willing to do everything necessary for your ultimate survival on Planet Blue. I AM WILLING TO GIVE MY LIFE FOR YOU, MY PEOPLE!" After this, I hear and feel more unity from the crowd as they begin supporting my plan. I finish my speech and proudly recite our Planet's Creed:

"I trust the government of my people to protect me from any attack, alien or domestic. I believe we live on a unified planet that is based on long-lasting peace founded by our soldiers. That is why I love this planet and its Klithans. It is my duty as a resident of this planet to be a soldier first and protect what we have built and love."

The creed is well-received by the Klithans as they have a strong love for this planet, and I use it to my advantage to obtain their support.

My life has been devoted to protecting this planet, and today is the day I can do something extraordinary to fulfill my duty. This planet has been at peace since I was born, aside from the minor domestic skirmishes that have been part of our history since I was born into our forces. Now is my time to prove why I am here, and I am going to demonstrate that I can save this species from extinction.

It is time to take care of the remaining royal line, so I call on my daughter to take charge. "Aliza, I have an important mission for you. Right after the king's assassination, the royal children fled. Who knows where and what they are planning to do. I give you full responsibility. I trust you will take care of this inconvenience as best as possible."

"Yes, Sir."

As she leaves, she stops and turns around. "Thank you, father."

I appreciate my daughter, but a stern face is needed to encourage her to remain strong and stay focused on this mission.

Six

Born Anew - Jako

7:46 a.m.

What is this? I feel hot like a fire is running through my veins. But it is not an uncomfortable feeling. As a matter of fact, I like it. The power given to me by Liath is beyond my understanding. I am unsure of what abilities I possess, albeit I feel much stronger. I overlook my new physical appearance, but I guess I look pretty scary since my little one seems frightened.

Liath finished what she had to do, and I feel the urge to fight back well back up inside of me. Away from town, all the way to this forest, I witnessed the destruction and death brought by this species. I don't dare argue that we are any different since I am aware that we humans could possibly do worse. Perhaps violence is coded in our DNA or wired into our brains from birth, but so is compassion and empathy. We, humans, are far from perfect, but we learn every day. As a soldier

47

and as a warrior, I have pride. I'll fight back with everything I have. I will not stand down…I will not forgive. I clench both hands into fists.

Belisa notices this. She knows me too well. She can read me. She knows that I am about to go and look for this commander and challenge him. She quickly moves close to me from behind and encloses my fist with her soft hands. "Jako, I know how you're feeling, but you don't know what you are capable of. They might kill you if you go rushing to face them without any practice."

I know my wife is right, but I am sometimes stubborn, and I must do something right away. "Belisa, there is no time to train. I feel invincible right now; I feel I can take them all. The longer we wait, the more people will die, and I cannot let that happen. I have to do something now!"

As I say this, my body begins to feel hotter, and I see lightening around me. I look at my hands, and they seem to be surrounded by white fire. My body is ready to fight. And even though my brain tells me otherwise, my heart is full of rage. I turn around, softly caress Belisa's face, and kiss her. As I pull back, I see the worry in her eyes.

"Jako, you cannot leave us alone! You cannot go and just wander around looking for him! You promised to protect your family! So, we will walk together and come up with a plan to protect each other!" She is firm with me. She is right ninety-nine percent of the time, and I should stay close to them because they are powerless to protect themselves. But I have to figure out what I can do.

"Belisa, this is the only way I can protect you."
I turn around and run.

Suddenly I am in the middle of nowhere. I don't know how many miles I just ran in a short moment, but I am fast. I look around with a grin, and I feel excited. This feeling is inexpressible; however, my excitement is rapidly overwhelmed by reality. I am not sure where I am, but it doesn't matter since this part of the city is also destroyed. The only bodies I see are cold.

I turn around and run the opposite direction; I notice time slowing down. As it starts to drizzle, I notice each raindrop hitting the ground in slow motion. My face breaks the raindrops as I speed by. As I return, I see my family standing as if they were frozen in time. I run around them for a second, which, for me, feels like an hour. I stop playing around, and the look on Luke's face is priceless.

Astonished, my son Logan, exclaims, "you could probably defeat those aliens with your speed alone!"

Liath questions, "haven't you considered that some of us could be as fast or even faster than Jako? This is a very utilitarian power to possess, as speed is beneficial to elude physical attacks and for adding precision to your punches. However, the adversary could be faster; then, you will need to figure out how to overcome that disadvantage and make it work in your favor."

"Exactly my point." My wife points at me shaking her index finger. "Jako, you have no idea how powerful they are. You don't know your capabilities. Tell me, as a soldier, what do you think the outcome of a fight would be? You, of all people, should know that this requires preparation and analysis."

I know my wife and Liath are right. And I know my desire to avenge our species is clouding my judgment. I am a soldier, a man that must act quickly; I don't have time to think while in a crisis. I only have milliseconds to decide in a situation that could mean life or death. But also, that way of thinking can be counterproductive. I know I need the help of Liath to develop my decision making to minimize errors. After all, her species has generational experience. I could have just skipped thousands or millions of years. Who knows?

After a few moments of silence, crestfallen, I decide to acknowledge my wife and Liath's argument.

My stomach growls, I am so desperate for revenge that I forgot we need to eat.

Since we have MREs and we are far from the city, I tell Luke, "Hey buddy, you must be starving. Would you like to try what your father ate during his time in service?"

His eyes widen, and his face draws a big smile. "Of course, daddy, you know I would love to eat what you have. I would like to do everything you have done!"

Although I love what he says, I wouldn't want him to go through what I had to, especially during my time in Special Forces. I missed so many important dates, so many birthdays; I even missed his birth.

"Luke, remember to be your own man. I made my decisions and lived with the consequences. I am touched that you would like to be like me, but you should become your unique self. Be a good man, a good husband, but don't base your decisions on mine, okay son? Maybe you are a little too young to understand, but I know you are brilliant, and you will remember what I say when you are older." I hug him for a second and then pull back, grab a Chicken Pesto from an MRE box and give him to him. "One of my favorites!"

I tell Logan to start opening another box so everyone can pick what they want. "They are all good!" I say and laugh.

"How do we heat them?" Belinda asks.

"With water, but we don't have any at the moment. It has started to sprinkle a few miles away from here, and we will have plenty of water soon enough. Don't worry; the MREs still taste a little better than starving when they are cold." I say in a deadpan tone.

We are enjoying the meal sitting on the grass. We can see the sun rays hit the dark clouds of an incoming storm from the west, making their way to our location. I hope that what comes next is for the best.

Seven

First Encounter - Logan

8:13 a.m.

Here we are having a good time in the woods. I am enjoying this moment watching my family share what could be our last laughs. To be honest, I don't remember when the last time we actually sat as a family and had a meal together was. Maybe we did more often when I was younger, but not lately. My mother and my father are great parents, but we lack something. Perhaps it's because of my dad's crazy schedule and workaholism that we lack the communication a family should have.

But where do we go from here? What should we expect from this new life? Everything has changed, including the rules. We must adapt and survive. The enemy is of another race, their purpose? Their purpose is to conquer us through force. However, we were not part of their plans. They want total annihilation of humanity as we know it. Communication is the key to survival.

My father acquired a power that we do not understand. He, himself, doesn't even know his capabilities or limitations. He knows he can run fast, like really, really fast. Other than that, we are all clueless.

With my meal almost finished, I stand up with my MRE in my hand and walk towards my father. The others are minding their own business, lost in thoughts. As I get close, he stands up and looks at me, intuiting that I would like a word with him. He could always read me pretty well. Standing in front of each other, he asks, "You have an idea, don't you?"

I nod. "Yes."

he puts his left arm around my torso and leads us a little further away from the group. "Ok, I am listening."

"Well, father, I was considering the situation. I believe we are putting ourselves in a lot of danger if we keep wandering around. We need to find shelter. The storm is also getting closer. We need to make sure my mother and the kids feel safe and you...-"

"-Me what?"

"You need a safe place where you have time to train and master the powers within you to have a chance to beat the Klithans."

My father is very proud, and at times, he can also be impatient. Even with all of his training, he couldn't control his basic male instincts of using strength to do reckless things. I was praying his new power hadn't yet gone to his head.

He looks away, towards our destroyed city. "I think you might be right."

After our conversation, he looks at me and smiles, then starts talking in his Sargent's voice, "Attention every...-"

Before he can finish his first two words, the same phenomenon that happened at the military base begins happening right here, where we are eating. The air feels charged and tense, and a strange light appears to come from nowhere. My legs start trembling, my body temperature drops, and I start sweating. I know what is coming, and we are outside in the open. My dad looks at me and says, "Everything will be ok, son."

I believe him, but I still can't stop shaking. I feel my legs will collapse like a newborn horse. Why am I so afraid? I wish I was like my father, so fearless, always ready to take situations, people, and problems head-on.

"Logan, Logan!" My dad yells. "Come on! Snap out of it! let's go; we need to hide the family!"

I come to my senses and run with everyone to nearby bushes. We don't have much time, and the bushes will barely conceal us. My father is holding Minda's hand, and my mother holds Luke's hand. I am behind everyone.

The atmosphere continues to change. Fierce winds, lightning, and some sort of gravitational energy are lightly pulling our bodies. There is no doubt more Klithans are coming through.

Behind the bushes, everyone is huddled close, including Liath. Everyone seems afraid, but I am

54

the only one shivering. Five Klithans, as expected, cross the wormhole. Large and imposing, with textured skin in colors not seen on any human. Their faces seem stretched or distorted. They look so ugly. We would classify them as monsters since their features are not within our parameters of beauty. I turn to see my father, and he seems eager to fight them right then and there. He was waiting for this moment. My mom holds his left arm firmly because she knows that he wants this. He wants to go out there and challenge them, but it is not the time. It is not safe for him or us. I could see my dad's rage and his desire to fight in his eyes. However, I am uncertain if his willingness to fight is to test himself, to keep humanity from being massacred, or to protect us.

My dad's muscles begin to flex and pulse with heat after all that clenching. His veins begin swelling under his skin. His skin glows with whatever energy courses through him now, more and more. My mother is trying her best to calm him down, but she says that his arm is getting way too hot. She has to let him go. Unable to restrain him, his glowing aura gives away our position.

My father stands and faces the invaders. "Belisa. I am sorry that I couldn't control this. I will do whatever is necessary to win this fight. If I survive, I will train to learn how to control my emotions and how my body emits energy. But right now, this will be my first test. A trial by fire. Without arguing, find a place further away from here to hide. Take everyone…Including Liath."

Liath looks at my father. " Jako – "

"-GO NOW!"

My mother starts to run as the aliens make their way, slowly toward my dad. "Come on! Run! Hurry up!" She points out at a cave formed in a hill a few meters in front of us now. We are getting close to the cave, but I have to watch. I turn around to see how my father is doing. I can barely make up the scene. It seems as if he did something to fog the alien's vision so they could not see us hide. I can see five silhouettes. Five Klithans are surrounding him. It is five against one, and he still looks calm. Why is he so composed? I know he is confident, but they will try to kill him. Could he figure out how to master his new body and powers so quickly? I can't bear thinking of my dad dying. Inside the cave, I urge Liath to help my father. I grab her by her sides and shake her. "You have to do something." I keep nagging. "You have to help my father."

"Child, I –"

My mom grabs me and gets between Liath and I. "- Logan, Son, I know you are afraid for your father's life and ours as well. But you have to trust him. I know sometimes he can make some hasty decisions, but let's remember that he has special training for any situation. His orders were to run away, including Liath. I am certain he had his reasons."

I look down with concern, and my mother, along with Luke and Minda, come over to hug me. I can't stop shaking. I am not ready to assume the role of "man of the house." However, if something were to happen to my dad, I need to keep it together for my mother and my siblings.

Liath walks slowly until she nears the cave's entrance and says, "look, they are about to start fighting." We all hold hands, look at each other, and peer outside fearful of the pending brawl.

Eight

Loss - Alizabeth

Planet Klith: hours before the invasion.

I am proud to be under my father's command. He deserves his new title as King. I look up to him. And though he wants to act cold-hearted, I would like to think he loves his only daughter.

Since I was young, our relationship has never been normal. I don't really have much knowledge about him, about his past. My father's priorities always focused on his work. I would like to think that I was mature enough at an early age to understand.

He loved my mother. His attitude was different before the tragedy happened, and my mother had perished. I am certain that's why he has changed, grown distant. Now that it is just him and I, and even though he loves me, he is afraid to show it. Perhaps he thinks it would be easier this way in case another tragedy comes to pass, and he loses me. He shelters his heart from feeling too deeply.

I am his only child. So, it is up to me to make him proud. And I will.

My first objective is to kill the Queen's children before they jeopardize our mission. I have never killed before.

It baffles me why Liath and Lioneth would oppose our plans to conquer Planet Blue. After looking at the earthling's history, it is evident that they would not accept diplomacy and co-existence. They are a ruthless, primitive species that only knows how to enslave, kill, and destroy. It doesn't matter. I will find and kill the children. I could put them away with their mother, but that would likely cause more trouble.

A soon as my father commands, I hasten toward the cell that holds Liath. I know that would be the first place they would run. I wish I had the speed of other Klithans, that would be convenient.

On my way to the cell, other Klithans are preparing to leave. All of them shapeshifting into what humans would see as monsters, but each and every form compliments our individual strengths. Large size, horns, thick skin, and more; we are perfect weapons. There is no need for armor; we have learned their technology, strength, and weaponry are no match for us. Because of our superiority, we will be perceived as Gods to their naïve minds.

Everyone is, in my way, saluting me. I am my father's daughter. I have no time for that nonsense, but I refuse to look arrogant in front of our people. I return gestures, recognize admonitions, giving my best wishes to those leaving. I ask if they have seen the Queen's children, yet no one has.

The corridors in our underground fortress are well-lit, with lighting throughout. Every tread nosing on every step is illuminated. There are no dark places, nowhere to hide. You could not see your own shadow. *How is it possible that no one saw them running?* The advanced abilities of every Klithan are different, and I am unaware of which skills they may possess.

I reach the door of the cell, which is still closed, but I am unable to see inside. I raise my hand to activate the DNA scanner, which unlocks and opens the door. The cell is empty. I curse and begin thinking; there are no signs of an escape. The entire system's database was reprogrammed, allowing only us to activate the door. One of the children must have the ability of molecular oscillation. I have failed, I should have known. They could be anywhere. Moving through walls is a beneficial skill. My mission is getting out of hand. I do not want to disappoint my father, but what do I do?... What would the Queen do? Where would I go if I was her? My husband was just killed. I was opposed to Commander Danteloth's plans. The answer reveals itself: She will warn them all. She will ruin this for us; she will work against us. They are going to travel to Planet Blue. I yell as my fists crash against the cell wall.

Could they intend to ally with the species on Planet Blue? It is a possibility, and I cannot let that happen. I enter the travel room. Everyone looks the same now. Our purpose is to frighten and attack—

the probability of finding them just decreased. I must take ahold of myself. I must think patiently, yet quickly to deduce their location. Maybe they would be eager to leave. Perhaps they will wait for the precise moment, but when?

As I think, I analyze everyone, playing close attention to their movements, their behavior, until I notice something; A group of three Klithans is acting somewhat nervous, different from the anxiousness from an imminent invasion. It has to be them. They have not noticed me yet. I begin walking stealthily towards them. I am closing in just as a group is getting ready to leave. Five Klithans walk to the center of the room, and the wormhole opens through the energy manipulator. The wormhole grows and begins to displace the light in the area, it is almost ready for the group to enter as it happens; The three make a run for the wormhole. One spots me and says something to the other two. He lunges for me and tries to fight to buy time for the other two to flee. I run to try to stop them from leaving, but the brave one, perhaps the son, tackles me hard. I fall on my back, but as soon as I feel the floor, I use my momentum to launch myself back to my feet and grin.

I am a warrior, born, and bred. Although I have a mission, fighting unfailingly excites me.

My father taught me the traditional art of Klithan fighting. This art focuses and enhances a fighter's strengths. My strength is in my legs; therefore, I mastered all lower body techniques. Though I know I am fighting a mere child, I don't hold back. I deploy my strongest fighting stance.

61

I run towards him and slid tackle him using my legs as scissors to bring him down. I feel the floor tremble from his hard fall. He is shocked, and I take advantage of his pause to swing my right heel down into his stomach. I push myself upright and return to my fighting stance. He shifts back to normal and, as I had thought, it is Liath's son. I notice a grin on his face; he lets out a defeated chuckle. I am perplexed. "I did it. My sister and mother will not be treated like criminals at the hands of traitors."

I wait to respond. I let him enjoy his hope a moment longer. "I am so sorry to disappoint you," I reply, "but your little sister did not make it. She was caught before she could jump with your mother. And trust me, this won't be tolerated by the new King. You will be executed for treason. You and your family are obviously against the best interests of our people. It is inexcusable that you would prefer to save another race over your own."

His expression changes dramatically as his grin fades. He slowly stands up, wincing, with his hand on his stomach where I had hit him. As he straightens, he looks at me saying, "Danteloth, your father, is not our king, and will never be. He is a disgrace to our people and to all we live for. The way he is executing this is not right by any standard, and you know it."

One little part of me is listening to his claims, but with everything happening, it is too insignificant. I move close to him, lean into his shoulder, and whisper in his ear while I look at his sister, "die knowing you could not do anything to save your sister." And before he could turn to see

62

his sister's eyes for the last time, I stab him through the heart. His body drops to the floor and his sister, while detained by the soldiers, yells, struggles, and cries. They are a menace to our people, just unable to see what they are. I approach Liath's daughter, and she tries to say something. Before she can, I slice her throat. The soldiers let her go, and her neck lurches backward as she falls.

My mission is incomplete. The queen has escaped, and it is my fault. I had plans. I have to consult with my father.

"Father, I need a word with you."

He does not turn around. "What is it, Aliza."

"Father, forgive me. I have failed to complete the mission you gave me. The queen has escaped."

Frighteningly calm, he replies, "and the children?"

"They are dead, sacrificed their lives for their mother. I could not forgive their actions against our people."

This time my father turns around upset. He already returned to a more subdued form. I can see it on his face. Thick brow furrowed into a frown, fiery bright blue eyes, and thick lips surrounded by a long beard. "Aliza. You do not take such actions without my consent. What if they had information that could help us?"

I reply quickly, "father, one of them has the ability to vibrate their cells through any solid surface. We could not take any chances."

My father was not pleased. "Alizabeth, you have no experience in this situation. Consider this your first and last mistake. We cannot afford to make any more at a time like this."

He turns around and does not say another word. It was my cue to leave the room.

My father is tough. He has always spoken his mind. That is one of the things I respect most in him; not many are as blunt as he is. I had no chance to tell him I was planning to follow the queen to Planet Blue and redeem myself. Perhaps it is better this way. I will just return to him with Liath's head.

Nine

Untold Power - Jako

8:15 a.m.

On my ability to fight back with this new-found power, rests the fate of the entire planet. Talk about feeling overwhelmed. My family's life depends on me. I have to keep focus and fight with all I have to force them to leave, at least this area to keep Belisa and my kids safe.

I am already surrounded by five aliens. They look like demons. Blackish skin and red pupils surrounded by darkness. Horns, big muscular arms, and forearms with veins that lead to big hands with elongated fingers with long, sharp nails. Their legs are muscular, standing as a goat would.

My body is tingling. It could be fear, anxiety, stress, adrenaline, perhaps everything together. But believe it or not, I am ready to fight. I have years of combat experience. In my mind, I can take them. It doesn't matter if they have had millions of years of evolution to their advantage. I know I have more heart than their entire planet combined. I must. I am the only one capable right now of stopping them.

They form a circle around me. I raise my hands in a boxer's pose, demonstrating that I am ready to fight. They start to look at each other and share a gesture and a human-like laugh that echoes into the forest.

"What are you laughing at?" I ask.

One alien in front of me says, in perfect English: "Your arrogance amuses me. Do you really think you can defeat us? We have had studied your race. You break easily. You are, mmm... what is the word I am looking for... you humans are brittle."

"Why don't you bring your ugly ass over here, and I will show you how brittle we are? I point at him. "I will crush you with my bare hands." And I make a fist.

I am ready.

The alien I am exchanging words with runs towards me. I can see him running in slow motion. He isn't as fast as me. I am able to see everything in a fraction of a second; I can read his movements. When he is close enough to throw his first punch, I can see it coming and have plenty of time to elude it.

I avoid the punch, and the momentum from his overconfidence throws him off balance, and he tumbles to the ground. "What the hell just happened?" He shakes his head, puts a hand on his knee, and gets up.

One of his slender fellows slowly walks towards me, eyes suspicious. "He is able to move like some of us, very fast. I saw him because I can do that too. Let me take care of him."

"How is that possible?" Another alien says, "he is just an earthling. Although, this one has a different appearance."

I smile and direct my voice to the one that can move as fast as me. "So, you want to take me down just by yourself?"

"You are arrogant, indeed. That's going to be your ruin. I am one of the fastest of my race…if not the fastest Klithan."

This is my opportunity to take out all of them. If I can get the others just to observe, they will not notice my family hiding. I have to bide time and make sure they don't spot them.

"Ok, lets fight. Tell your subordinates not to interfere. I will take care of them after you." I say.

"There is no need for them to interfere." The alien extends his right arm in front of his chest and clenches the fingers into a fist.

The plan is working just fine. I'll kill this one, and the others will have no chance against my speed.

The other four aliens move with a jump a few meters away from us to give us space and observe the fight.

The alien ready to fight is glaring at me, he is about seven feet, and I am merely five feet and ten inches tal-… Wait, no, I'm not. I hadn't noticed, but the world seems a bit smaller. What the hell? My height is now almost a match for these monsters; our eyes are nearly level. His presence is intimidating, but it doesn't scare me; I am now larger as well as faster and stronger than I was. I am eager to show what I am made of. I am anxious to show that this is my planet, and they will not succeed because I am here to protect it.

In an instant, without any words, without any warning, he throws his first punch. I can see his big fist with sharp knuckles coming and barely elude it. He is fast. There is one more punch coming with his left hand, and it hits. It really hurts. I can feel his knuckles penetrating my right cheek. It feels like getting hit by tons of iron at tremendous speed.

I have no time to avoid it, and he sends me flying meters away. He is not just fast; he's strong as hell. That punch makes my bones vibrate, and I have a feeling that wasn't at his full strength. I might be in big trouble here.

I start to get up. He is already in front of me. My eyes widen, my mouth slightly opens, I just cannot believe how fast and strong this alien is.

"Clean the blood from your lips," he says as I stand up.

I lift my arm to the corner of my lips, and with the back of my hand, I rub it. I look and at my blood and think that I am no match for him. However, I have to keep going; it does not matter how strong they are. I'll be stronger and protect my family.

"Do you want to give it another try?" he asks.

"Of course. I will keep fighting until I cannot move." I get into a fighting stance. "I am the only hope of this planet."

The Alien also takes a fighting stance. "Let's go."

I run with all I got towards him. I don't see him move, and I trip and fall hard on the floor again. Still, on the floor, I use my arms to lift my upper body and turn around. He is standing there. He tripped me, and I didn't even see him. *Am I done here? Is he just too fast? Is my power not enough?*

"You are not what I expected, I admit. You are highly above average. However, you are still weak. Stronger than the average human but still human. You are no match for me or others that are as fast as me. You have to surrender before I wreck you."

I can't stand the idea that I am the strongest on this planet, and I am being toyed with by this alien. I am being tossed around like a used rag. I am supposed to be the hope of this planet. If I cannot beat one single alien, how am I supposed to defeat an entire race?

I get up and turn around. Looking down furious, I mutter, "You come here to my planet, and wreck it with no warning. You come here and kill who knows how many people…" I turn my hands into a fist. I slowly start to raise my eyesight until I see directly into his diabolical eyes and yell… "You will pay for what you have done! For all that your people have done! This is not over! I can do this all day!"

I gather all my strength, and I start running. He stands still. I can see him move slowly. I throw my first punch at his face, and he is too slow to avoid it. He is recovering from that one, but my second punch is a hook with my left fist going towards his abdomen. He tries to block it, but I am so furious my punch goes all the way crashing his hand against his stomach. I keep hitting him with a series of combos, jab-cross-left Uppercut-overhand right repeat. He stands no chance. A gush of dark blue blood comes from his mouth. I keep hitting him as fast as I can and end it up with left jab-jab right-cross. I stop, and he is still standing. I use the "Spartan" kick in his gut, and he goes flying against a tree, and it breaks. He is on his knees. The other four aliens are looking at him with concern.

Making sure they don't see me. I look quick at the cave where my family and Liath are hiding. Belisa seems concerned. With a furtive hand gesture, I signal her to calm down. I really have to take these aliens away from her before they see my family.

One of the aliens witnessing the fight says, "you are going to pay for this. We are thousands and you-"

"Everything is alright." The alien I am fighting interrupts him while getting up. "He had a little push from his emotions. Next round, I will finish him and continue with the plan."

He walks towards me as if my combo of punches did nothing. "Hey, I would really like to know what your name is," he says.

"Why?"

"You are nothing like the other humans. I want to know who is the one giving me this nice welcome to this planet."

I stand quiet.

"If you won't tell me your name, I will get it out from you by force. You will feel so much pain you will beg me to stop."

"Ugh, you definitely don't know me, big horns."

He starts to get annoyed. "Do you think that because you made contact, you can hit me again? I underestimated you. You had an emotional boost. Now that I know your limits, it will not happen again. Do not test me."

"I tell you what. Let's go to more open space so we can fight more comfortable. This is just starting to be fun. I am getting excited."

"Alright. I'll follow you. But you better give me an enjoyable time, Earthling."

"Your friends. They cannot run as fast as we do. How are they gonna follow us?"

"Do not worry about that. Linth has the ability to instant-transport. He will take the rest wherever you bring me."

II hope Belisa waits for me and doesn't do anything crazy. I know she is smart enough to do the right thing in this situation.

I turn around. "Alright, follow me."

We run, and I notice everything is also destroyed on the way.

I stop at some open barren field far away in the middle of nowhere, and the other aliens appear in an instant.

"Why do you want to know my name? The real reason." I ask.

He looks away and chuckles, then says, "to be honest, I haven't had this much fun in years. You are not only fast, but you are strong. I wonder what other abilities you possess."

My blood, I can feel it warming up my body. "This is fun for you!? Killing innocent people!"

"Innocent people?' Human, you are not innocent. You all, as a species, are repugnant. We are doing this because we must. There is no time for negotiations. But enough of this! You will tell me your name or not?"

"My name is Jako, The guardian of this planet."

"Guardian? You are not a guardian. I am not stupid. Even if you are, it would be a disappointment."

"What do you mean?"

He starts ambling around me. "On my planet, there was a queen…"

My heart skips a bit… *does he know…?*

"This queen wants everything done in peace, but your race is not peaceful. She loves diplomacy. She wants to coexist along with your race. After fighting you, I concluded that she is here. And that she contacted you." He looks at me sharply.

"A queen from another planet that her race wants to kill us. That travel through time must have damaged your brain."

He stops his walk, and throws a scrutinizing look at me, "I never said I traveled through time. So, she is here. I heard rumors that she had the ability to evolve species, but I never believed it was true."

He dashes against me. I can't see him. I just feel a very painful kick in my stomach. I can see his quad muscle so close in my face, and I spit blood. My body is in shock.

"Well, Jako, 'the first guardian' I wanted to have some fun with you, but if Liath is here, I bet the commander will have a good reward for her head. Rest now and give me a good fight next time. Tell Liath she will bear the same fate of your species. By the way, my name is Klatoth."

His knee unscrews from my gut, and I fall to the floor.

Ten

A Stranded Child - Belisa

8:53 a.m.

I wonder where Jako lured the aliens too. He is always trying to protect us, even if it might kill him. The fight seemed balanced. However, I know it was not. The alien he was fighting took no damage from his attacks. I really hope Jako is ok.

Minda pulls my blouse. "Mom, is my daddy gonna be ok?"

"Yes, sweetie, of course, he is gonna be just fine. Did you see how he attacked the alien and went flying against the tree? Your father is a strong man and now even stronger. He won't ever give up that easily."

Luke gets closer. "Mom, why did my dad leave us alone?"

"Papi, your father did not leave us alone. He took the aliens away from here, so they can't find us and hurt us. He is just fighting them in another place. As soon as he is done with them, he is gonna be back right here with us…ok."

The kids have strong hearts; however, they are still kids. I have to be stronger for them and be prepared for the worst.

Jako has been gone for a minute, and I have no idea how long to wait or what to do. I guess the only thing I can do is wait as long as needed.

The cave is cold, moist, and rocky. It smells like petrichor. The smell reminds me of the beautiful rainy days in which sometimes I would go outside with the kids to enjoy the natural phenomenon. The smell of the wet ground brought me peace; lost times, when we were happy, and we never really worried about anybody else. Perhaps that is why Jako is so passionate about fighting these aliens.

Jako's biggest dream is to help humanity and leave a legacy. He wants to create something, be an inspiration, have a helping foundation. Instead, he got stuck with a wife and three kids. But that's just how I feel. He would never tell me otherwise. I know he loves our children and me. But I know how deep inside his dream still sleeps, waiting to be awakened.

Logan is at the mouth of the cave, peeking his head out to see if he can notice anybody. I run towards him, and I reach for his right shoulder from behind. "What do you think you are doing, Logan?"

"I am just trying to see if my father is coming back, mom."

"You should know better. If some of those aliens see us, we are done. Even Liath is not strong enough to protect herself or us for that matter."

Logan walks back to the deep of the cave and leans against the rocky walls. "I am sorry, mom. I am just nervous, scared, and worried about my father. I don't think he is gonna make it."

Liath walks and approaches Logan. "Logan, look at me. Your father is a strong human. More so now than ever. When I was in the 'evolutional ritual, I could feel how strong his heart is and that Logan will make your father always stand back up and surpass his limits."

I walk towards Logan and take Minda's and Luke's hand on the way. When we are all together in a little circle as a family, I say, "Logan, Luke, and Minda, all of you should and will always trust your father. He has always had so much faith in all of you, and now he needs you to have faith in him. When he is not here, I will protect you with my life. I will do my best for you three to survive -"

A sound interrupts my inspiration.

"Mom…" Luke hugs my leg so hard I would need a tool to peel him off. "…did you hear that?"

It sounds like steps approaching. I quietly put everybody behind us and backward, step by step, walk to the deepest wall of the cave.

I turn my head slowly and raise my index finger in front of my puckered mouth. "Shh, nobody says anything," I whisper.

The steps get closer and closer. Sounds of crackling bushes accompanied them. I really hope it is not an alien, if it is, we are doomed.

Liath steps outside of my protected perimeter, and she gets in front of me. "I will protect you."

Now that Luke and Minda have seen the aliens, they are terrified, and their body language is radiating just that. Logan is having a tough time controlling his fear as well. They are shivering.

The shadow of whoever is outside is just by the entrance of the cave. The shadow shapes horns, and it is big, can it be? Liath gets ready to fight with what it looks like a kickboxing fighting stance. I am also prepared to fight. I am ready to give my life for my kids.

Where are you, Jako?

A human hand grabs the edge of the cave's entrance, and the rest of the body shows. It is a man, a short young man that looks a little older than Logan wearing a peculiar Vikings hat. He has not seen us yet. We are in the darkest part of the cave. He reckons with his sight what he can see of the cave. He does not see us and comes in. The young man sits down on a rock. Liath looks at me with doubt about what to do. I keep analyzing him. His clothes look dirty, his skin and forehead shine with sweat.

Minda steps wrong on the floor, and he hears the noise.

"Who is there?" He gets up quickly.

Before he runs scared, I decide to come out of the darkness, protecting us. "It is just us...humans."

"How can I trust that?"

"What do you mean?" I ask.

He backs ups close slowly to the exit. "I saw aliens morphing into humans. Those monsters can be anybody."

"We are not them; I swear."

"Prove it." He takes a step back.

"Ok, I will prove to you I am not –."

"No, no..." He points to all of us. "...All of you will prove it from there."

"Son, think, if we were all aliens, we could have already killed you. And think, why would we be hiding in this cave."

"I don't know the stupid alien's agenda. Just prove it."

I look at Liath. *How can she prove it?* To give us some time to think I will prove all of us first.

"OK, did you see any of them bleed?"

"Of course not. I did not have time to fight them, you know...?"

"Then tell me, son, then how are we supposed to prove you we are not aliens?" I ask.

The front of his right foot starts hitting the floor rapidly. "I don't know, lady. Better think of something!"

Luke behind me says, "wait, what if you are the alien and you are trying to bring us outside to your friends and eat us.?"

"What? Kid sh—

"Watch your mouth in front of my children, young man. This makes no sense. This is how it's gonna be. We can't prove either of us is an alien, but let's look at the facts. You entered this cave looking for a place to hide, which tells me you are not an alien; you are lost. You found us here hiding from the aliens in this cave. I am just a mother taking care of her children, and that should be enough to trust us and us to trust you, agree?"

He agrees to what I say, nodding his head and sits back down.

I can't stop thinking about Jako. I know he is gonna make it back, and we will wait here. We have no other option.

This young man looks like he has been running for a while and seems hungry. Perhaps he could help us get the MRE's we left when the chaos of the aliens arriving happened. He and Logan are the youngest and fastest in this little group. It is risky but necessary.

The strange boy is playing with a twig he got from the bushes, drawing on the moist ground. I waste no time and approach him. "Hey, what is your name?"

His head still down while he keeps making hieroglyphics. "Why do you wanna know, we won't last enough in this place to be introducing each other."

"Hey, I just gave a speech to my kids of how not to lose faith, and I'm not about to do it again."

He looks up. "Then what are you doing right now?"

"So disrespectful."

"Look lady…-

I point at him. "-No, you "look," You can't be going through life-giving up so easy. That's what is wrong with this generation. My husband is out there fighting five aliens, and you are here sitting on your butt, questioning what is the point of introducing each other?"

He stands up again and throws away his twig. "What!? Your husband is fighting those monsters by himself. Does he have a death wish? Everybody should be hiding right now." His eyes wander away, "Not to be a coward, but we are not strong enough."

Luke doesn't stay quiet, "my father transformed into a superhero."

The guy starts mockingly laughing as Jako runs inside the cave, leaving a trail of white light like a comet behind him that, after a few seconds, disappears.

The young man's mouth drops to the floor.

"I told you, my daddy is a superhero," Luke says.

The young man is picking up his mouth from the floor stutters. "Who are you, Sir.?"

"So, now you are interested in introductions, ugh?" I say.

Jako turns around to face him. "My name is Jako."

"Are you some kind of God, Sir.? should I kneel? Is it true that you are her husband?"

"No, I am no god. I am just a regular human that evolved. And yes, I am the husband of this beautiful woman," Jako says.

"Ok enough with the drooling and tell us your name," I say.

"Yes, ma'am. My name is Shum."

So, suddenly he is so respectful. He must be so impressed to see Jako that his personality changed drastically.

I turn my attention to Jako. "Jako, what happened? We were so worried about you. We have so much faith in you, but there were five of them."

He grabs my shoulder with his firm and warm hands. "Yes, B. I am fine. I couldn't defeat them, but for some reason, they spared my life. And they know Liath is here."

"What? How?" Liath asks.

"They knew I am not a regular human since they studied us before coming here. But it was my fault. It slipped my lips that you people travel through time."

Shum's left-hand covers his mouth. "Wait a minute; you are an alien?"

Jako looks at Shum, and Shum looks away and lets him continue, "as I was saying, I mentioned that your people traveled through time, not just space, and that's when he connected the dots. He knows you are here because he knows the rumors you have the talent to evolve organisms to their maximum potential."

Shum asks Liath, "you can do that? Can you do that to me too?"

"Do you play any sports or meditate?"

"I play FIFA."

Liath looks confused at all of us. "What is FIFA?"

"Shum, just…be quiet for a second," Logan says.

Jako continues, "I don't know why they let me go. Perhaps I should say why he let me go. What was his name again…Klatoth."

Liath backs up, and her face freezes. "Did…you…say… Klatoth?"

"Yes, that's the name. Why? What is the deal with him?"

"Klatoth is the strongest Klithan there is, and you survived a fight with him. He never shows mercy. He always kills whoever is in his way. I am perplexed. Why would he let you go if you are a threat? He must be planning something."

"Whatever it is, I believe he enjoys fighting with strong people. Right before he let me on the floor, unconscious, he said he would like to fight again, that I should get stronger to be a challenge to him. That I was one of the strongest, he ever fought."

I still had in mind the MREs. That is food that we will need to be strong and be able to run and hide when needed. We require that food. So, I tell Jako to go and get it as fast as he can. He comes back, and I offer some to Shum.

"Are you hungry, Shum?" I ask.

"Yes."

I throw a Chicken Pesto MRE to him. "There you go."

We all watch him desperately rip it out of the box and eat it cold.

I don't know how long we are gonna be running and trying to survive this invasion. But as long as we are alive, we have to keep hoping for the best, appreciate the little things and be humans to each other.

Eleven

Last Sight - Danteloth

10:03 a.m., Planet Klith

My daughter can be just like her father. And it is certainly both annoying and delightful. After killing Liath's children, she took it upon herself to go and look for Liath to kill her as well. She is so devoted to me and to this invasion. Nothing could be more satisfying than taking Liath's life with my own hands. However, seeing my daughter bringing me Liath's head would be just as pleasing.

I wonder what is going on right now. I need to be there. I sent Klatoth to take care of things until I get there, but Alizabeth can be a little stubborn.

We are about to send to Planet Blue all Klithans that survived the rise in temperature before we could finish the facilities underground. Not everybody made it. Millions died. We will not be able to withstand the heat rising more.

I am getting anxious.

"Come on. Hurry up; we cannot be here forever. We have thirty more Klithans to send, and I can already feel the temperature rising by the minute. We need to hurry!" I yell at everybody.

"Commander, I mean My King, you should go on the next iteration, we all will meet you there. In about two hours, we all will have crossed."

"Tell me, soldier, what kind of King would that make me? I will wait until all of my people cross. Besides, my daughter and Klatoth are there. I know the mission is in good hands. I have to see everybody cross," I reply.

I am not leaving this place until every single Klithan crosses. This is my duty. I can be seen as a mad man by many, but if it was not for me, we would have been still here wasting our time, waiting for death. I cannot forgive Liath for favoring Planet Blue's interests.

I walk to the room where we have special suits to go on the planet's hot surface. I open the door using the retinal scan. The system echoes "access granted," the door opens, and I walk in. I really want to observe what was our home for so long. I walk towards the purple and white suit and press the green button placed to the right, halfway up in the locker to open the door, which is keeping it enclosed. I grab it and look at it, thinking that this is it, the end. I unzip the front and start putting it on one leg at a time. Next, are my arms on the sleeves and finally my helmet. I zip it back up and grab the oxygen box from the rack. One arm goes through one loop made by the straps and then the other. I connect the oxygen, read the levels to make

85

sure everything is in order. I start to walk outside the locker room towards the elevator that will take me to the surface through the lonely corridors that remind me of how lonely my life without my wife has been. Nostalgia makes a flurry of thoughts whirl in my head, but I keep walking. Tears start to wet my cheeks. I have to be strong for Alizabeth. I will not lose her like I lost her mother.

The walk to the elevator is not that far.

I get to the elevator, and the A.I. states the temperature on the outside, "three hundred and fifty degrees and rising on the surface."

Our suits are made to resist four hundred degrees. It is risky, but I really want to see, for the last time, my lands.

I say, "open," and the elevator opens its doors. I walk through and hear a mechanical sound announcing the door closing behind me. I do not turn around. The elevator gets all the way to the top, and I say open again. The elevator opens the doors facing outside, and I can feel the heat. I walk out slowly. The suit can barely take it. I just want to observe for a few minutes. I walk one step at a time watching the landscape and the sky. The land is just a big desert; the planet is starting to turn red. The star that once gave life is killing it, and we are part of the genocide. It looks a lot bigger; it is expanding trying to swallow Klith, my planet.

Are we really the last of the species in this universe? We could not find more life, and the universe is also dying. We thought the Universe had more time. The accelerated expansion will ultimately be the universes doom. Humans are a young race, perhaps the first race to inhabit the Universe. That is why they have not seen the entire potential that life offers. They are blinded by greed. They do not deserve the planet they live in; they are also killing it.

But what is going on with my suit? I can feel the heat getting into the suit, that is impossible; this suit should last at least an hour...unless...

I start to race back. The begin to plod back; as my suit melts, and the boots are starting to glue against the surface. This suit is already heavy as it is. It is taking a lot from me to lift my feet in every step. If I continue like this, I will also run low in oxygen. This is getting scary. I am starting to think that the A.I. gave me incorrect information. This temperature must be higher. There is no way the suit should be melting. I look at the thermometer on the suit, and the temperature is close to four hundred seventy degrees.

I need to hurry up, or I am going to be baked out here. I am looking down, and my boots become slime, keeping me sealed to the ground. I use all that I have and take one step. I came to see my planet one last time to say goodbye, and it wants to take me with it. I refuse to die this way. I raise my eyes and look at the door. The light is blinking, announcing somebody is coming up. I cannot walk, I am stuck, I fall to my knees, and my head hits the floor.

Twelve

Stuck - Jako

10:03 a.m.

I am flabbergasted by how much faster Klatoth is than I am. That really hurts my ego. His knee to my gut will hurt for the rest of my life. My power is not enough, and it won't be enough if I don't train.

"Liath…Do you think you can train me? Train me the way Klithans fight?"

"Jako, I am sorry, but I do not possess any knowledge of combat. It would be better if you train with your own people, don't you think? Klatoth specializes in hand to hand combat. If you learn our way to fight, he will be able to read all your movements."

I flex my right arm up to a ninety-degree angle and make my hand into a fist. "Where am I supposed to find somebody to train me? Your people are slaughtering humans left and right."

Shum finishes eating, throws the MRE bag on the floor, and stands, "Sir-"

Belisa turns her sight to Shum, "You are on everything, aren't you."

"Call me, Jako, kid."

"Ok. Jako, I know something…"

"…Well?"

"You see before I found your family and that…alien…I was part of a group heading to an underground military camp for refugees. Maybe, just maybe, there is somebody on that camp that can train you."

I walk towards Shum. "Wait a second, were you awake at the begging of all of this?"

"Yes, Sir. Weren't you?"

Logan says from afar, "we go to bed pretty early."

Shum mocks us, then continues, "well, the attacks started somewhere around 10 p.m. in this city. I was out at a Frat party-"

"That would explain that silly hat," Logan intercedes.

I stare at Logan. "Let him finish. This is important."

"As I was saying, before being rudely interrupted." Shum throws a glance towards Logan. "I was a frat party at the University of Sintlan when these five aliens came out of nowhere and started killing everybody. But it wasn't just killing you know, it was a massacre, slaughtering all my friends.

89

The only thing my mind told my body to do when the adrenaline hit was to run for my life. So, I did."

Crestfallen, Shum stops telling his story.

"Kid, you did nothing wrong. I am trained to kill, and perhaps I could have done the same. It is in human nature to fear what we don't understand, what we can't control, or simply just looks scary. But we need you right now. I am rusty on what I learned in the Special Forces, and I need to train this body. I am not completely sure of what I can do."

Shums eyes start to water as he looks up and says, "I know, but perhaps I could have helped, and all I did was run. Everybody is dying, and I just ran."

"Shum, nobody is here to judge you. We all have done things we regret. You just did what your survival instinct told you to do. Survive. If you did not stay to fight, it is because your mind and body are not ready. Perhaps you are meant for something more, and that's why you are now alive. You have to find a purpose. Train with me. Become stronger."

Shum's watery eyes light up with hope; he uses his forearm as a towel to dry his tears and continues. "After I run for, I don't know how long, I encounter a military convoy on Highway 55 going south, and they picked me up. When I was on that convoy behind a big truck, there were a few others. I hear on a soldier's radio that they were heading to the underground camp the government has been creating just for this kind of situation. A few minutes after that, I heard a soldier yell, 'Incoming' and everybody panicked. I jumped outside the truck, and the front of the convoy was getting attacked by those monsters. Guess what I did again."

"Let me guess…you run?" Logan mocks Shum.

I look at Logan. "Logan, what would have you done?"

Logan stays quiet, and I contemplate some options.

How can we find that camp? The only info we have is a convoy going south on 55. I am the only one fast enough, and we have two little kids.

"Does anybody have any idea of how to go about this? We need to get to that camp?" I ask everybody.

Everybody looks down, trying to come up with a solution. The silence in the cave is loud, and no ideas lighten our day.

I walk to the mouth of the cave, and I look up. I gaze at the sky, and I see it getting covered by the darkest clouds I have ever seen. A storm and a strong one is not far. Could this play in our favor?

I feel Belisa's soft, tiny hand reaching my shoulder from behind. "Jako, I don't know what to do. I have no idea what to tell you. I am scared to go outside of this cave."

I turn around to face her. "B, to be honest, I am also scared. The alien that I fought was powerful and faster than I am. We need more people that can become whatever I became. I won't be able to win this fight by myself. But one thing I will assure you.

I will die first before any of you get hurt. That is a promise."

Belisa looks into my eyes and hugs me firmly, putting her beautiful face against my chest. "Jako, just hold me and tell me everything's gonna be ok?

I comply, "everything is gonna be ok, mi amor."

While Belisa and I are hugging, Logan approaches us. "I think I have an idea."

Belisa pulls away gently her resting head on my chest and replaces it with her left hand; she looks at Logan. "Let's hear it, son, you are the brains of this family, tell us what you got."

"Well, mom, my father is the only one fast enough to outrun most Klithans since not all of them can run fast. Liath told me that they all share different traits; some are fast; others can go through walls using molecular oscillation, etc. So, my father could recon the area a few miles south from here and find another hideout, once he finds it, he comes back and one or two by two he could transport us at super speeds over there and just like that we keep moving."

"Son, that's a good idea." Belisa unwraps her arms from me. "Jako, do you think you could do that?"

"I am pretty sure it is possible. Hopefully, I won't get all my stamina down."

"Jako, you are very new to this body. This new body will be demanding more energy than it can supply. It is a risky tactic," Liath says.

I understand precisely what Liath is saying, but do we have other options? I don't feel fatigued from fighting Klatoth; then again, I barely fought him. *What should we do?*

"Liath, do you have any other skill besides evolving other species?" I ask.

"I only have that ability and share the ability to shapeshift with all other Klithans."

Minda raises her hand with her face expressing excitement. "Daddy, daddy! I have an idea."

I walk towards her and keel right in front of Minda. "Go ahead, sweetie, what is it?"

"Well, what about Liath transforms into one of those monsters, and act like we are all her captives. That way, you don't have to waste your energy."

"That could work!" Logan says.

I stand up and ask Liath, "we got two ideas. What do you think? Would you be willing to take the risk, transform, and act like we are being dragged somewhere?"

"This is also my survival; they are also looking for me to kill me. It could be a good idea if you did not fight Klatoth yet. He is probably spreading the word that I am with humans, and if they find us, that could be our demise."

We have no other option but to try Logan's idea. Liath is right. Besides, she is the only one capable of evolving more of us to fight.

I tell Belisa I love her and give her a kiss like it was the last one I would give her. The stakes are too high. I tell everyone not to get close to the opening of the cave or even crane.

I run.

Rain is falling, and I see every drop suspended on the air before my face breaks them. I feel like I will never get used to this. It just looks so unreal. I love this.

I pass a few Klithans at high speed, and they can't see me. Some can feel the trail of air I leave behind, but that's about it. I keep running south on highway 55, and I can't see anything, no place to hide. I keep running. There are only barren, open fields in highway 55, scarce shrubs no taller than Minda.

I come to a stop and notice the storm getting worse. Thunder is louder than atomic bombs near your eardrums; lighting is so rapidly fired by the dark clouds that it illuminates the fields like concert lights. My little kids must be terrified. I need to go back and think of something else. There is no way I would transport them anywhere in this storm.

I turn in the direction back to the cave, and I prepare myself to run back. But before I can move one foot, something strikes me. It burns like hell. It feels like some sort of energy travels through my entire body. I feel charged. I have the urge to unload energy. *Did I just absorb lightning?*

My body gets warmer, and I feel tingling on my hands. I lift my hands to waist height, and I see sporadic sparks surrounding them. The tingling intensifies, and I extend my right arm in front of me with my hand open and watch how bluish-white energy discharges from my palm. I destroy a mound about one hundred meters from me.

The tingly feeling subsides.

What just happened? How did I do that? Can I do it again?

There is no time right now to figure it out; I have to go back and quickly. The storm is becoming very bad.

As I prepare to run back, I feel a sting on the back of my neck. I reach it with my right hand, a bright green, almost glowing dart.

I start to feel weak.

After a few seconds, another sting. I grab it and throw it away. I feel weaker. My legs can't support my weight anymore.

Another Sting. Son of a-…

Thirteen

Liath's True self - Logan

12:43 p.m.

I am so tempted to do what my father emphasized, not doing. I want to crane over the opening of the cave. I am curious. But I won't risk us all.

I have no idea how my little brother and sister are taking a nap, just resting their heads on my mother's legs. My mom is caressing Luke's and Minda's heads, passing her fingers through their hair while she gazes into nothing. Her gaze screams concern. She is apprehensive about what could happen to my father. However, she also trusts him.

He is taking too long. Not sure how long has passed, but I am guessing a couple of hours, at least.

It is so dark outside because of the crazy storm. It is hard to tell the time. Lightning light reaches the mouth of the cave but is not enough to reveal that we are inside.

Liath is sitting down with her legs crossed, and I wonder how she really looks. Would this be the right moment to ask? Perhaps I could ask her to transform while we wait for my father. Although I really like the way she looks like a human. She looks so shy, inoffensive, and frail. I don't know if I wanna break that cute image.

Shum is standing with his arms crossed, looking at the entrance of the cave, moving his right foot up and down like he has restless leg syndrome. I am thinking about getting to know him since we might be stuck together trying to survive this invasion.

Before I make any attempt to talk to him, he looks at me and approaches. It is like he read my mind.

"Hey," he says.

"Hey." I nod.

Shum leans and murmurs, "so, how old do you think Liath is?"

I can smell alcohol in his breath. "How would I know?"

"Well, you have been hanging with her for a few hours."

"Well, in her human form, she looks around sixteen."

Shum smiles and looks at Liath with a deviant look. "I know, right. She is so cute."

"What is wrong with you, man? We are in the middle of humanity's extinction, and you are thinking about that?"

"Hey, with more reason. It could be my last…you know?"

"She would be underage. You have no moral code."

"Guy, she is the queen of another planet. She is not sixteen. Although I would not mind if she stays in that shape while-"

"-Shum, just shut up!" I turn around, and I walk away towards Liath. Perhaps a bad idea to make conversation with a dumb ass.

When I get close, she can feel my presence and looks up. I smile and ask, "may I sit next to you?"

"Of course." She taps twice with the palm of her left hand, the empty space on the rock. "There is more than enough space."

Liath has intrigued me since we met her back by the bar. She went from a cute, frail girl to a queen trying to stop a galactic war between two worlds. I really wanna know how she looks for real, but I don't know if it is right or not to ask.

Liath gets closer to me and says, "I don't know much about human emotions. However, I know that all living things have feelings. One can tell from a gaze of a simple physical movement that something is preoccupying someone. Even in an animal's gaze, we can tell it's sad, happy, or scared. That said, I know you want to ask me something. That is my sixth sense. And I am sure I know what it is."

How could she possibly know what I want to know? Is it possible that she can read my mind?

"No, I am unable to read your mind."

"But I didn't say-"

"I know, I am just kidding. I took a guess of your thoughts. I just guessed right," she says and smiles.

"You are hilarious." I fake a smile.

"Logan, you are different. You have a good heart and that I can tell by just looking into your eyes. You also have a curious mind. You would like to know how I look as a Klithan, right?"

Am I that obvious?

My heartbeats are getting faster.

I stand slowly, and she follows. "Well, Liath, now that I know that you know what I want to know. Yes, I would like to know. I am just curious."

My mom, the kids, and Shum heard the conversation, and they get closer. They have been curious as well. It is just natural; it is who we are. Liath tells us to stand a few feet back, and we move.

She looks down and raises her arms towards the sky in a ritual-like movement, and her shapeshifting begins. Her body is visibly morphing into a taller shape. From around five feet to six, no, seven feet tall. As her arms slowly start going down on her sides, her skin color begins changing; a shade of pink, with some gray in, it's the best way I can describe it, but it keeps changing. The shape of her body is just like a woman from this planet. Her hair starts growing. However, her hair is thicker, a lot thicker than human hair, and it grows all the way to

99

her waist. Her skin finally settles into a beautiful shade of red. Her body resembles everything from a human. But her skin covers her private parts. It is like her skin is self-aware.

As she starts looking up, her eyes are similar to ours, with the difference that her eyeballs are more prominent, and it is hard to tell the color. It is like a universe that is inside them. Her eyelids blink sideways. Her nose is so delicate and tiny. Her lips are like a work of art. She is beautiful in her own way.

"This is the real me. This is who I am as a citizen of Klith." Her voice changes a little. Just more mature and soothing.

Luke and Minda were just out of words looking at her, and my mom didn't know what to say. Shum, on the other hand... "Hey, down here." He waves at her like a dumb kid. "Wow, girl, you are huge."

I can't take his attitude anymore, and for the first time in my life, I hit somebody. I walloped him Shum goes down, and my knuckles hurt like hell from crashing against his jaw.

Shum is on the floor, kneading his jaw. "YOU ARE DEAD KID!" Shum gets up furious, tries to hit me, and I feel the hand of Liath on my chest while she gets in front of me, between Shum and me. Liath picks up Shum from the shirt and brings him to her height. My siblings start to laugh while Shum comically squirms to get out of Liath's grip.

Liath brings Shum closer to her face. Shums feet are about two feet up from the floor. "Stop acting idiotic and immature, or I will throw you so far away that the other not so kind Klithans find you, are we clear?"

Shum stops struggling and looks down. "I am sorry, ma'am."

Liath puts down Shum and asks us, "so, what are your thoughts? Not what you expected."

My brother is the first one to answer. "I thought you would turn green and have antennas."

We all start laughing. Even Liath gets a kick of it.

My mother then says, "forgive my kids. They watch too much Television."

"Television?" Liath asks, confused.

I try to explain, "Really, there is no Television on your planet? Perhaps that is why your race is so advanced. Television is a square box, well now it's not so much a box anymore. The point is that television is the invention that slowed down our advancement. It's full of senseless entertainment. You can sit down for hours and watch the lives of other people that don't really matter or watch men fighting for a ball to score points and make millions while doing it, etc. Anyway. Not important."

"Well, this is me, but I would like to go back to my human shape, so you don't feel too uncomfortable."

As Liath starts changing, my mom starts questioning where my father is. "Logan, your father, is taking too long. I am sure something happened. I can feel it."

"Mom, my father is one of the strongest out there. I am sure he is still looking."

My mom's voice aggravates, "Logan listen to me. Something is wrong. We need to do something. Your father got in trouble. Us women can sense stuff. It is hard to explain."

"But mom, what do we do. We have no power to win against any of them."

My mom grabs me by the shoulders strongly and tells me, "come on Logan, I know you can come up with something. Since you could talk, you came up with the greatest, most ingenious ideas or solutions for any bad situation you were in. Please, son, do it for your father!"

Fourteen

Liath's Plan - Liath

6:24 p.m.

I wonder what happened to my children. I am certain that if they got caught, they are already gone. If Danteloth's ideals are adamant, it is indubitable my beloved children perished in the hand of the commander or his offspring.

He murdered my husband at a close range with no regrets. He had trained his daughter to resemble him.

My heart hurts… my chest feels like it wants to burst. My entire skin feels warm and tingling. I am laden with pain, but there is nothing I can do while being here, and there is no way to go back.

If Aliza even touched them, she will feel the wrath of an entire family.

Right now, I am tagging along with some very kind humans. It seems like Danteloth lied to me when he said that this race hated each other. What else could I expect? He just wants to fulfill his ideals in his own way. And one way or another, he is succeeding. My husband is dead, my kids are not with me, and he is the self-proclaimed leader of my people. What do I have left?

I think about what happened every second. My husband, Lioneth, did not deserve to die the way he did. He was the nicest Klithan I have ever known, and he is gone.

My stomach is churning.

Jako, the human that I evolved and is supposed to save this planet, is not here yet. His evolution was incredible. He has many traits mixed. I felt a hidden power coming from within him even before he morphed into his new body.

Klithans have only one unique ability. However, we all possess the potential to shapeshift. We all have strength, speed, and stamina way above the average human. At this point, I only see Klatoth as a challenge to Jako, and therefore, it is strange that he is not back.

It is exhausting to wait in this dank cave.

The storm is starting to calm, and we really need to do something; Jako is not coming back. Something must have happened. I have to talk to Belisa. They all seem too afraid to go outside, but we have to.

I make my way to Belisa and ask Logan if he can watch the kids and give me a minute with his mother.

Logan grabs the children by their hands, and as they walk away, Logan tells them, "come on, Luke and Minda, grownups need to talk."

It must be strange for Logan to say that when I look sixteen.

I turn to Belisa. "Listen, Belisa. It has passed plenty of time. We need to face the facts. Jako is not coming back, and we need to go out. I doubt that Logan will come up with a good idea when he is so scared. Unfortunately, he is not the kind of person to make these decisions just yet. He is too young. He lacks the experience necessary to lead a group of survivors. He must be clever; I doubtlessly believe you. However, I question his character to command."

Belisa's expressions agree with my statement and have no argument against that.

"Belisa, we need to do something. It is in our best interest to move out of this cave because we will be found. Our best bet is to take the risk and go South; head to where Jako ran to and keep going until we find him, or a clue of where he could be."

Belisa looks at her children the way I would look at mine if they were in their position. She loves them so much, and one gaze says it all. "Ok, Liath, do you have a plan? Or we just walk outside and pray we don't get caught by those monsters?"

"Please, I ask respectfully to not patronize me."

"I am sorry, Liath. I am just so worried about my husband." Belisa's eyes display sadness.

"Belisa. I cannot think of another way. We just must be careful. We have to walk stealthily, be aware of our surroundings at all times, and hide if we see or hear something suspicious."

Belisa swings her gaze to me. "What, that is really our only option. We should wait I know Ja-"

I interrupt, "Belisa, I know the idea may sound a little vacuous. But Jako would be back by now. Something is not right. He is so fast he should be back, and he is not"

"It is getting late. We should also rest through the night to have strength for the upcoming days. Trust me, they will be long days. We have food here, and only one person has found this cave. Jako already fought around here. I doubt they will look in this area at least for a while."

Belisa makes a valid point. Most of this horrible day is almost gone. We should rest. So much has happened and the stress in everybody is high. However, the kids and Belisa have been unreasonably calm for this kind of situation. Perhaps they went through a similar experience before. They worry about Jako but not to the point of craziness. They seem to trust Jako will be ok. Maybe his military career was hard, and it made this family more unified.

"Alright, Belisa, I agree. We should probably eat something and get some rest. We still have those boxes with meals ready to eat, but we will be out after tomorrow's breakfast. So, if Jako is not back by dawn, we have to start moving."

Belisa responds, "ok. Let's gain some energy back" She turns to the kids. "Hey Luke, Minda, let's eat something and rest ok. We have a long day tomorrow."

Those kids are so lovely. They obey everything their mother orders. They are such a great family so much trust. It reminds me of my family. And I cry inside. I might not have that back ever again. I miss my children.

Everybody clasps one of those meals and starts eating. I grab one and walk to the other side of the cave. I just want a moment alone to think about my family while I see Belisa's family unified in the hard moments. At the end of the day, we are not so different at all.

Fifteen

Renaissance - Jako

8:03 p.m.

Damn it. What did just happen?

I squint my eyes. I start looking around. Everything seems so blurry. My head is spinning, my stomach is churning, and I feel like vomiting. I can barely distinguish things. White walls, metal lockers to my right against the walls, the lights are incredibly bright, so bright I can't stop squinting my eyes.

I am lying down on a table.

What the hell?

My hands are locked to my sides with a metal band around my wrists. My sight travels over my legs to my feet, and they are also fastened. My boots are gone.

What in the hell am I wearing? Some sort of blue scrubs.

I squirm in the table, but it is impossible to set myself free.

Did I get captured by those bastards?

God Damn it. I am supposed to be the one to fight them, and I get captured this easily. I need to get out before they kill me.

"Hello… can you hear me?" A female voice, soft and confident, echoes through the walls. "Who are you? And why did you come to our planet? Is this a genocide?" do you need our resources?"

Well, now I know I got captured by humans, and that is more embarrassing.

"Whatever you are, whatever your name is, respond to the questions, or there will be consequences."

"What kind of consequences?" I lift my right eyebrow.

There is silence for a moment.

"We are not playing around. The table you are locked into is electrified. One flip of a switch and your body will be electrocuted until we get answers from you. If you are not one of them, you have nothing to worry about."

I laugh and the say, "well lady, you can tr-"

My speech gets interrupted by a charge of volts traveling through my body. Apparently, I cannot absorb this electricity, and it really hurts. "Stop, stop!"

"We don't have the time to play games. Now that you know we are serious…Who are you?"

"Alright, alright. My name is Jako. I am human. I am on your side, …obviously. I have fought against the aliens."

"Oh, really, you are human?"

"Yes, I am. Why wouldn't you believe me?"

"I am gonna ask you again…Jako…" her voice resonates doubt. 'What is this attack about. Why are you aliens attacking us? We have done nothing."

"Ma'am, I am telling you the truth. I am human fighting this war as well. I have three kids and a wife that must be worried sick about me. You have to let me go."

"Jako, we saw you. What you can do no other human can. You have abilities humans don't have."

I start recovering my vision. My eyes keep investigating the room. "I can explain that."

"Oh, really? Well, I am listening, Jako."

As I look around, I notice a camera that is on the top left corner of the room, right above the only door and another one on the top right on the wall facing that door.

"What is your name, ma'am?"

"That is not important, Jako."

"Come on. I am tied to a cold metal table. I can at least have your name."

"Stop stalling and explain yourself."

"Ok, ok. Long story short. We met a good alien. She is fighting with us to stop this war. She has the power to bring the full potential of species, evolve them, and she did that with me."

"So, you're saying that you are the evolution of humans."

I smile. "I am so glad I don't have to explain myself twice. You are smart, lady."

"I am not sure if I should believe you, so we are going to run a simple test. We will need you to give us a blood sample Jako."

"So, you want me to pinch myself and give you blood?"

"I am so glad I don't have to explain myself twice," she says.

I gotta admit… she has a great sense of humor.

"Why didn't you just take a sample when I was unconscious. It could have been a lot easier."

She clears her throat. "You don't know, do you?"

"I don't know what?"

"Jako, your appearance changed while you were unconscious lying down. Your hair changed from glowing white to black, and your extreme muscular size went down a bit."

I don't know what to say. I thought I evolved. Liath said my appearance was unchangeable. I am so confused. Did I lose my powers? Can I reaccess them? Damn it. This is not good. So frustrating. Well, at least the kids won't be so afraid of my looks anymore.

I try to keep calm and look to the camera by the door, and with a gaze, I point to my locked hands. "Would you please unlock my extremities, so I can do what you ask for?"

"I will, but please don't try anything stupid. This room is equipped to take down anything dangerous with a push of a button. Understood?"

I nod in agreement since I know they can see me. The metal cuffs around my hands and feet unlock. I sit down with my legs hanging on the left side of the table. I look up to the camera by the door. "Is there any way I can get a mirror?"

"Jako, you can get anything you want as soon and as long as we identify you as human. Now walk towards the lockers, and in the first drawer, you will find a barrel syringe, a hypodermic needle, gauze, tape, alcohol, cotton swabs, and a tourniquet. If you are who you say you are, you should have no problem doing this. Would you like to walk you through, or do you have the knowledge?"

"I'll be alright."

I raise my right hand, reach the handle, open the drawer, and grab the tourniquet first. I set it around the bottom of my left bicep very tight. I grab the barrel syringe with the right hand and the needle with my left. I thread the needle to the barrel syringe, take the cap off and slowly stick it on the vein with my right hand. I set the tip of my thumb right under the plunger flange to push the plunge back and get the blood. I take the band off my arm to let my human blood flow. After a few seconds, I pull syringe off, put the cap back on the needle, set it down, and grab the alcohol swabs. I use the swabs to clean where I stuck the needle, grab the gauze and tape to cover and elude infection. I breathe heavy the entire time. I hate needles.

The same voice echoes inside the bright room. "Alright, Jako, thank you for your cooperation. I will be in contact as soon as we know who and what you are."

What is this place? It looks like something the government would build. They always have a secret agenda the public is ignorant of. Society is always oblivious to what doesn't affect them directly.

I wonder about Belisa and the kids. I don't even know how long it has been. I really hope they are alright, I left them alone, and if something happens to them, I won't be able to forgive myself.

"Jako." That voice again. "Jako Pineda, we know who you are." The door opens. "Please join us."

I don't say a word and start walking towards the door. I look at the camera on top of the door, and it follows me. I am a foot away from the door, and all I see is darkness.

"Please, Sir." A different, high pitched voice resonates in the corridor. "Just keep walking. The lights will turn on as you walk."

"Sir?"

I start walking, and bright white lights turn on in front of me. I turn my head around, and I see the lights in the room I was in turning off. As I keep walking, lights keep turning on. The corridor is plain white. The floor is cold.

I approach a door, and when I am close enough, it opens. A red-head lady is waiting for me with my bootcut blue jeans, my tan jungle boots, and a white cotton shirt, in her arms.

"Sir, I am sorry for what we did to you," she says, standing with my clothing still on her crossed forearms.

"Do not worry and stop calling me Sir. I prefer for you to call me Jako."

She smiles and lowers her head, "ok, Sir…" She nods, "…I mean, Jako."

"What should I call-"

Another woman intercedes, "you should call her Lizi. And you should call me Miss Magna." She extends her right arm for a handshake and looks directly into my eyes. "Mr. Pineda." Her handshake is firm, and she seems well educated. Her eyes resemble that of a lioness; her voice is soft but imperative. She looks relatively young, probably in her late twenties. She is beautiful. Her blonde hair in a ponytail and not much makeup, just a little red lipstick. I wonder where she ranks in this facility. After a few seconds, she gently pulls her hand, turns around, and starts walking away from me, saying, "Mr. Pineda," she points with her right-hand index finger. "Please use the bathroom on your left to change clothes. We have work to do."

"What? Work to do. First of all, what is this place… I have a family to get back to, Miss!"

She turns around quickly. "Mr. Pineda-"

"Please, just call me Jako." I look around and see five men working on computers. "Everyone, please! Just call me, Jako."

She sets her right hand in her slim waist. "Very well, Jako. Do you know the severity of the situation humankind is facing?"

"Yes, I know. However, my family is out there by themselves. My wife, my six, eleven, and seventeen-year-old. Defenseless."

"I know this alien you mention earlier is with them, right? And I assume she should also be strong as the rest of her race."

"I don't know that for sure," I reply.

"Jako, even if you wanted to go save them, you can't. Don't you remember?" She points at the mirror a few feet away from her. "Look."

I see my reflection from afar. It is me, The powerless Jako. I don't even know where I am. And my family needs me. But if I go like this, it would be suicide. I need to unlock my power again.

"So, Jako..." Miss Magna calls for my attention, "...we have a training room where you can train all you need to unlock that power we saw earlier when we captured you."

"May I get something to eat first. I am starving."

"You may get anything you need. You should also rest, Jako. Your body has gone through some huge changes in a brief period of time. You need to rest to replenish your body and mind to be able to train focus."

"I will right after you tell me, what is this place?"

"Very well. I will keep it short. We are running out of time. This facility is one of its kind. I named it 'Renaissance.'"

"Renaissance," I mutter.

"Yes, Renaissance. I named it that way because it was built with the sole purpose to assure the survival of humanity against any odds."

"Wait a minute…" I look around. "…If you named it, that means that you pay for it to make it, not the government?"

"That's right, Jako. I tried to convince the government to build something like this in every state just in case of a cataclysm, or any rock out of orbit that could hit us and end life as we know it. I was denied the funding; they thought I was out of my mind. That it would take so much money and useful resources from realistic projects, but look at us now. I know the president is regretting his decision. I am a wealthy woman and took it upon myself to build this enormous underground bunker slash refuge. It's top-secret, and only those who were involved in building it know about it until now. I never thought that an alien invasion would have marked the end of us. But that's enough for now; you need rest. We need you. We will find your family, I promise."

Sixteen

Who is Miss Magna? - Jako

DAY 2, 3:00 a.m

An alarm sound fills the air and travels through it to drill my ears. The beeping sound is so loud and annoying that my body is reacting without my brain being in total control. My eyes widen. The bright lights hurt my eyes. I squint.

With a blurred gaze, I see the drab ceiling.

I am in a room that looks just like a white cube furnished with a shiny metal desk, a black swivel chair, a metal frame where my hard mattress is, and a digital clock that seems part of the wall that reads three in the morning in green numbers.

I am used to waking up at this time. I cook my meals before heading to the gym at four fifty a.m. However, this time I feel exhausted. I feel worn out. Perhaps this is my body rebelling, not being used to the power and transformation I suffered and lost.

I need to get that power back.

Every single fiber in every single muscle is sore. And I can still feel the pain from the fight against Klatoth, although anybody who saw that fight could argue that I was nothing more than a punching bag for him. I was absolutely no match for the alien. I need to train to gain my power back, but that won't be enough. I also need to train to get faster, stronger, more powerful than any of them.

Still, on the bed, I swing my legs, reaching the cold floor with my feet. I lean forward and set my elbows on my knees while my fingers interlock and use them to rest my chin. I start thinking of a plan, a method to bring my powers back, and I notice the pillow they provided on the floor. I certainly threw it to the floor while sleeping since I hate pillows. They hurt my neck.

I have no idea how to regain my evolved form. My mind is lost in despair, distracted, worried about my family. I can't concentrate.

No ideas come to mind. I look under the bed and grab my boots. I put them on, stand up and walk towards the black swivel chair where I left the white T-shirt on to put it on. All ready and with my hair a mess, I walk to the door, and it opens.

Lizi is there waiting for me in her fancy black suit. Tiny, short, around five feet three inches tall, with fashionable red glasses. She must be in her early twenties. She acts very timidly around me.

"Sir-"

I put my hand up. "Lizi, what did I say?"

"I am sorry, Si-… I mean, Jako." She blushes. "I am here to take you to breakfast."

"Alright, Lizi, lead the way."

She turns around and starts walking. I follow.

As I walk down the corridor, which looks the same as everything else, white and bright, I can't help but wonder about Belisa and the kids. I really hope they are fine.

"Don't worry, Jako. I am sure your family is going to be ok. As we speak, there is a team looking for them," Lizi says as if she could read my mind.

"How did you know I was thinking about them?"

"Anybody should be able to read the face of a person when he or she is worried about something, especially family. We must have empathy for each other."

It seems like it doesn't matter from what universe, time, or planet females are; they can see emotions with a pure gaze.

Looking away, I reply, "I guess you are right." I return my gaze to Lizi. "What time did they leave, and how do they know where to look?" We take a right and keep walking straight. I have no idea how anyone can know their way around here; it is worse than a maze.

"They left right before you were woken up. They have a pretty good idea of where to look. They will start where they saw you and captured you."

I stop. "No, they made a huge mistake."

119

Lizi stops and turns to face me.

"I ran far away from them looking for a military facility, which I believe is this one."

Clueless, she says, "sir... Jako, they shouldn't be much further away from where you left running."

"Lizi, you don't understand. At that moment, I could run faster than sound, I believe."

Lizi starts laughing then says, "you are joking right. Nobody can run faster than sound."

"Perhaps you were not there when they brought me in and interrogated me. I didn't look like this. I was evolved into something else. I had powers."

She notices my face is pretty serious, and hers goes straight. "Oh, you aren't joking."

We keep walking, and she doesn't say one more word until we get to the door of what I presume is the Dining Facility (DFAC) "Jako here we are." She uses her fingerprints on a scanner to the right of the doors to open it. The door opens slowly. The room is massive. It is an amazingly spacious room.

I gape at the sight.

Like any other part, I got to see so far from this facility the color of law is white. Shiny metal benches to sit down and eat. The set up resembles that of a buffet with a big beverage line in the middle of the dining room.

The dining room is filled with uniformed personnel. This is the facility Shum was talking about. An underground base, but when and for what purpose exactly was this built?

As I look around, I spot Miss Magna gazing at me. She is sitting by herself having breakfast. I nod, she doesn't. Instead, she raises her left hand and uses her index finger to command me to walk towards her. As I walk, I notice soldiers looking at me as any fan would look to a retired celebrity. I don't mind the spotlight. However, Miss Magna said the government wasn't involved in building this facility.

I arrive at where Miss Magna is sitting. "Good morning, ma'am."

Miss Magna stands up and shows her right hand for a handshake. "Good Morning Jako. How did you sleep?"

"Well, considering that my family is stranded in what is now a war zone and that my ability to do any damage to my enemy is limited due to my powers being gone and I worry about the entire planet's existence...you could say I slept like a baby."

Miss Magna chuckles and says, "I see. You have a sense of humor."

"Where is this room in which I could train."

Miss Magna sits back down. "I knew from going through your records that you were an exceptional member of the armed forces, and that is why the military asked you to join the Black Jaguars. However, it is a whole different thing to see that attitude in person. You haven't changed at all. You have kept your motivation, discipline even

121

after your military career. And I respect that. But for now, sit down and have breakfast with me. I know you have plenty of questions."

"I joined the military for a reason and with a belief. The belief that as a soldier, I must maintain and exceed standards. As a soldier, I must be outstanding in everything I do, outworking everybody to show excellence. As a soldier, I always need to be physically and mentally prepared. This should not stop when a soldier ends his or her contract with the military. It should be carried on."

I didn't notice that the soldiers were paying attention to our conversation and that my voice was echoed throughout the dining room. When I was done with my speech, one by one, they begin to clap.

I look around, and I feel a sense of pride. I am getting pumped up to train and become even stronger.

As the claps start to cease, I gaze at Miss Magna and say, "I will get my breakfast now, and when I come back, I would like honest answers."

I walk towards the food lines, and the soldiers in front let me go first. I keep quiet while I grab my tray, plate, and silverware. While going through the food bar, I grab the best possible, boiled eggs, oatmeal, two pieces of wheat bread, and a banana is just what I need to start my day and train hard. I walk towards the beverages line just thinking of Belisa and the kids. I grab a glass of milk, put it on my tray, and make my way back to where Miss Magna is sitting down.

I arrive at the table, set my tray down, sit down, and start eating.

Miss Magna slides her tray aside with the empty plates and dirty silverware. She wraps three fingers around the handle of her cup of coffee to bring it right in front of her.

I feel her eyes judging.

She is about to take a sip from her cup when I look up and ask the simplest of questions, "What?"

Before the cup of coffee arrives at her lips, she puts it back down. "Aren't you eating a little too fast. I mean, I know back in basic training you had to but not right now. You can relax."

My blood starts to boil as soon as she says that. "Relax…?" My right fist hits the surface of the table, and the trays tremble. "…Really!? How do you have the nerve to say that to a man whose family is out there with those damn monsters killing whatever moves."

"Jako, I am sorry you are right. I just-"

"I am gonna finish eating. After that, I will ask questions, and when we are done, you will take me to the room to train. I can't waste any more time. My family depends on me. You might not have noticed yet, but this world depends on my powers being restored. This enemy is more powerful than you can imagine. Even what they consider their weak ones are way stronger and faster than any of us."

I don't take more than six minutes to finish my meal. I put the tray with dirty dishes to my left and

123

lift my arms, setting my elbows on the table and interlocking my fingers. I fix my eyes on Miss Magna's with an unwavering stare. "What is this place, really?"

"Wow, you are going straight to questioning."

"Ma'am, I told you I am not wasting any more time."

"You didn't believe what I told you yesterday? Alright, then." She takes a sip of coffee, leaving her lips printed red on the edge of the white mug. "This facility was built with one purpose in mind…to survive from whatever global disaster may come. To protect from anything that could put humanity at risk of extinction. Believe it or not, this facility was not built by the government. This facility was thought and was made by private investors."

I laugh and say, "please, do you think I am an idiot. I am sure the government is behind all of this. And all your said 'investors' are the ones paying a ticket to get in here and save their own selfish necks. Look at all these soldiers.

"Jako, you have it all wrong. The government thought building something like this was a waste of money. A lot of rich people in this world care for humanity. Not all of them are the same. One of these investors had the idea and called some for a meeting. Those who she could trust and knew were going to agree to build this place. And look at this place now. If we did not have this, humanity would have perished for sure. At least now we have a fighting chance to survive, to preserve our species."

"You still haven't told me who are you?"

Lizi's voice comes from behind me. "Jako Miss Magna is the highest investor and therefore the owner of this place. She had the idea of building this with total civilian control. The armed forces you see here are working with us; we don't work for them."

This is incredible. Miss Magna should be in her late twenties or early thirties, and because of her, this is possible. My face should be radiating astonishment at this moment.

Miss Magna stands up. "Jak,o, I believe that what has been said is enough,h, and I know firsthand you don't tolerate the waste of time. Follow me; I will show you the particular room in which you will be training."

We walk through more corridors and take an elevator down one more floor. We exit the elevator, and I keep right behind Miss Magna and Lizi. We walk straight forward a few meters and get to another door. We stop.

"This is it, Jako. This room is specially built for intense training," miss Magna says

I am skeptical. "Do you really think that if I gain my powers back, this room could handle the training?"

"You will be surprised," miss Magna replies.

Lizi opens the door, and it is indeed another room so big and open. Shiny dark and bright, with protected mirrors all around. Around the perimeter of the room, there is regular exercise equipment while there is a vast empty space in the center.

"Jako, this room has plenty of equipment, gadgets, and technology. The regular public doesn't know anything about it yet, and you are not ready for it either. You will be ready when you gain your powers back. For now, focus on that."

Miss Magna starts walking away, and Lizi stays behind, looking at me. "Lizi, let's go."

I just stay amazed at the place I have for myself to train. I feel like a child with new toys.

Where do I start? How do I bring back this power Liath gave me? Will my body remember? It would be so much easier if she was here.

Seventeen

Liath's Fate - Belisa

3:02 a.m.

I wake up with a lot of pain from the unbearable position I had to sleep in to accommodate my little ones comfortably on my body, so they didn't have to suffer. I squint my eyes, and my head hurts. What time is it? I remove my stiff, left arm carefully from the bottom of Luke's body to try to see the time in the watch that Jako gave me on our tenth anniversary. The one I rarely take off. It is so valuable to me. He tends to forget important dates. However, I understand his brain is always daydreaming and busy. That is why it is so precious when he remembers.

Three in the morning? Jako's schedule really has affected me. It is way too early for us to be up, although it could also be the perfect time to move. The aliens already passed by over here. They probably moved on.

I look around, and I see a silhouette close to the entrance of the cave. I get scared and move stealthily. I, quietly, removed my right arm from under Minda's body and set her head on the floor carefully, so she doesn't wake up.

Whatever it is standing there hasn't heard me.

I lean forward as slowly as I can, and I carefully put my hands on the floor for support. My heart starts beating faster. I start standing up, and as I start looking up, I can see that silhouette eyes shining, looking at me.

"Mom, is that you?" Logan's whisper calms my heart.

"Oh my god Logan, you almost gave me a heart attack. What are you doing up at this time?" I whisper back.

"I am sorry, mom; I just couldn't sleep. It is not comfortable at all. Besides, somebody had to guard."

"I guess you are right, but everybody needs sleep. A tired mind and body are more dangerous than those aliens."

"I know, but I need to step up. My father is not here, and it is my responsibility to take care of you and my siblings."

Logan is taking responsibility, and that really impresses me. I never saw him as a leader, as someone that would step up and take charge. But I guess that when it comes to family, to defend what you love, we do things we wouldn't normally do.

"Logan, do you think we should move now?" I ask.

"Are you really asking for my opinion?"

I put my left hand on his shoulder. "Son, your father is not here, so you are the man of this family. What do you think we should do?"

Logan is dazed. "Well…-"

I raise my other hand to his right shoulder, "Hey, don't doubt yourself. A leader can't ever do that. I trust you, son."

"You didn't seem to trust me yesterday. I overheard your conversation with Liath."

"Logan, I trust you. Believe me." I nod reassuring.

I hear Shum, Liath, and the kids waking up, "What is going on mom, what time is it? It is still dark outside."

I turn around and walk towards the kids; my sight starts to get used to the limited light. "Hey kids, it is pretty early. It is around that time your daddy wakes up."

"Really, that early?" Luke says while rubbing his eyes.

Minda asks, "why are we getting up so early, mom. Has the storm passed?"

"Well, we weren't, but I woke up and heard something, it was just Logan. Then you guys woke up, although we were whispering. And yes, the storm has passed. I can't believe we all slept through it."

Liath walks closer to Logan and me. "Is there any plan for today? Without Jako's power, we will not defeat even the weaker ones."

I can see in Logan's face impotence. He wants to do so much for us but feels limited since he lacks the power his father has gained through Laith's ritual. Perhaps Liath should try on him what he did to Jako even if he doesn't practice any sport. He's a brilliant kid, and that might be enough.

Promptly I hear steps, multiple steps. We all hear them.

Liath says, "everybody quiet and go over there." Pointing to the darkest corner of the cave.

Logan is facing the entrance of the cave with his hands clench with the fingers doubled into the palm, and the thumb folded inward across the fingers. He is ready to fight for us. He is prepared to die for us.

"Logan, you too," Liath whispers harder.

The steps are louder. They are getting closer to the cave. We have no escape.

The kids, Shum, and I move to the corner. "Aren't you a little coward Shum."

"No, I am a survivor." Shum looks away, shameless.

Before I can say anything back, a man's voice comes from just outside the cave, "Is there anybody in there? We are a rescue team. We are coming in, don't be afraid, we are here to help."

Luke doesn't wait and, without hesitation, says, "yes! There are survivors here."

130

What the hell is he thinking? I pinch him.

The first man starts entering the cave, and as he enters, he begins transforming. It is like I can see them morph in slow motion. Luke, what have you done?

I stay back, and I put the kids behind me. Liath and Logan are paralyzed. A second alien enters already showing his real skin, and lastly, a girl that is with them. She must be an alien as well in her human form.

It is hard to distinguish how she looks entirely. She is around five feet four inches tall in her human form, and even though it's hard to describe her, I can tell, by her walk,she is in charge.

"I am looking for an Outlander that might have been hiding among you earthlings in a human form. She might have even told you our plan to eradicate human life and her plans to go against her own blood, her own race. And she could be you or you." She finishes her sentence pointing at Liath and me.

She walks in front of her alien bodyguards. "If you do not cooperate, there will be consequences. If you lie, I will know, and there will be consequences. Just tell me, is it one of you who I am looking for?"

There is silence. My kids are shivering. They are holding me so tight it hurts. They are terrified. Those monsters are about seven feet tall when transformed. Shum is petrified. I can't stop thinking about Jako and where the hell he is. Liath looks at me, and I can read her lips, "everything will be ok."

The alien girl walks away, towards the entrance, stops, and without turning around, says, "kill them."

"Stop Alizabeth," Liath says, "I will not let you keep hurting innocent souls. It is me who you want. Fight me and tell these traitors to leave them alone."

Alizabeth turns around with a grimace, "Traitors? You have the hypocrisy to call them traitors? These Klithans fought for you, and I…, I was training to become your protector. You are the one who betrayed us; you betrayed all of your race by joining forces with the humans."

"Alizabeth, do you really think this is right? Kill another species to save us? They don't deserve what is happening."

"My father explained to me all human history. They have killed each other throughout their entire history, and if they were in our place, they would have done the same. They would have killed us all without remorse. But enough talking. Your kids are dead, and now it's your turn."

Liath's voice changes. Her voice sounds angry, "What did you say?… You had the audacity to kill my children!"

Liath starts to transform into her original form. But this time is a little different. Her body is radiating heat. Her body starts to levitate. "Alizabeth, I will show you the true power hidden within me. Aaaaaaaahh," Liath starts to yell, and her heat increases. Something similar to what happened to Jako.

It seems like Liath needed to be pushed. And knowing her kids have died made her explode.

132

The cave is illuminated by this energy. I can feel warm all the way here, and I am a few meters away from her.

"What are you waiting for? Attack!" Alizabeth commands her subordinates.

The aliens try to attack, but Liath was already behind the two of them. She grabs both of their napes, stomps forward and smashes both of their faces against the ground. She pulls their heads, and two holes are made with them in the ground. She rises in the air, suspended in empty space while still grabbing their necks and flies outside the cave. Alizabeth follows, running, and I fall to my knees, and with my arms, I surround my kids.

Logan and Shum walk towards the exit of the cave and stand there watching outside.

"Mom, what happened to Liath," Luke asks, scared.

Before I can reply, Minda asks, "yes, mom, was that really Liath? She had powers like my dad."

"Yes, that was Liath, and I don't really think she even knew she had that in her."

Logan turns to face us. "Mom, come, Liath is fighting both at the same time. She is gonna win. The other two klithans don't have the speed or the strength to match her."

I tell Luke and Minda to stay back. I don't want them to see more violence and gore than they inevitably will see in this war. I walk towards Logan, and I start watching. The sky is so clear, and the moon so bright. We can see the fight distinctly.

Liath is dominating those two Aliens, and Alizabeth is just watching. Why would she not join the fight?

Liath's movements are deft and fast. All I can really see is the body of the Klithans twitching to Liaths hits. Suddenly both aliens are on the floor dead.

"Now, it's your turn Alizabeth, you killed my children, and for that, I will never FORGIVE YOU!" Liath's heat increases again.

Alizabeth remains in her human form.

"Transform and fight me in your Klithans form," Liath yells, while pointing at Alizabeth.

And out of nowhere, not too far from us, a bottle rocket sound-like effect is heard. Liath sees the missile too late. She gets hit by it. A big explosion goes off, and she drops to the ground.

Time freezes as we see a kind alien go down. We don't move from the cave except for Logan. I see him running and is already a few meters away from us. "LIATH," Logan's lungs give everything on that yell. Logan keeps running, and Alizabeth acts quickly. She runs towards Liath, pulls a peculiar long dagger that I have never seen before, and cuts Liaths head.

My jaw literally drops. I see Logan falling on his knees. Luke and Minda press their face against me, and Shum jaw also drops as he backs into the cave.

Alizabeth runs, and we lose sight of her. The moon is bright tonight but not enough to follow her with eyesight through the woods.

Liath is gone.

"Move! Move!" A man's voice orders.

Multiple steps approach quickly towards us.

"Ma'am, ma'am! stay there! Don't move!" The same voice yells from far.

As steps get closer, I get a better look at their uniforms: Khaki camo, and black combat boots. The ARMY has been fighting hard against this alien, and they are doing it non-stop.

"Belisa?" A Lieutenant asks.

How do they know my name?

"Ma'am, are you, Belisa?"

Logan is hysteric, furious after Liaths death, and he gets up from the floor and starts yelling at the Soldiers. "Why…How could you kill her?" She was on our side, and you killed her."

"What are you talking about?" The Lieutenant asks.

"The alien you killed was the only one on our side. She was the key to our survival. She had the power to unlock human potential, she had the knowledge of other alien's powers, and now she is gone because of you."

"How was I supposed to know that? She was attacking what seemed to be a human female. How could I possibly know? I saw a situation, and I reacted to it to the best of my knowledge, kid."

Liath's body is still lying there. Her blood is making a pool where her decapitated body lies, and the kids don't dare to watch. I keep their heads with

135

their eyes press against my body, and I, with a gaze, tell the Lieutenant to do something about Liaths body. Then I move my sight to Logan. "Logan stop blaming the soldiers for what it happened. They didn't know anything about Liath, and I assume they don't know either how they can shapeshift to what I think any species they desire to."

Logan's facial expression changes, from all-out anger to sadness. He looks at me with damp eyes, and then his gaze follows the soldiers carrying Liath's body away, so the kids don't see it.

I ask the Lieutenant how he knows my name, and he replies, "Ma'am, we were sent on a mission to find you and your family and bring you to a facility where Mr. Pineda is."

"Wait…Mr. Pineda, do you mean Jako…Jako Pineda?

"Yes, Ma'am, Jako is at this facility as we speak, training."

"Did just you say training? and we are out here about to get killed, and he is "training"? Training! Oh… no, Jako is gonna listen to me."

"Ma'am —"

"Stop calling me ma'am; you know my name."

"Ok, Belisa. I don't know what you expect from your husband, but even if he was an elite soldier back in the day, now he is a civilian and can't be out here fighting with us."

I chuckle and say, "you don't know, do you? You are just another soldier that follows orders, no questions asked."

136

"That is my duty." His posture radiates pride. "Enough talking. You can ask your husband everything you want when we are there. We need to move. We have a LAV very close from here, let's go."

Perhaps I hurt the Lieutenant's ego. I am just so mad at Jako right now; I can't help it. How can he be in the comfort of a facility, and we are stranded here? Oh, he will listen to me.

Eighteen

A Godly Meeting - Jako

5:03 a.m.

This facility is equipped with such technological advances that the public hasn't even dreamt of. This training room is immense. It has holographic combat simulators in which you can use a special suit to feel the hits you receive from an A.I Opponent. The layout can change depending on what you desire. Obstacles come up from the floor and walls to create different scenarios and add difficulty. And my favorite thing, just like Miss Magna told me, a suit that can multiply the force of gravity on the body, so that all muscles are engaged.

I still have no idea how to gain my power back. Is it mental? Meditating has never been one of my strong suits. It is hard to empty the mind and focus. Is it physical? is it spiritual? all together? As of now, I will just do my best and push my body past its limits. Perhaps that alone could do the trick.

I jump on the treadmill to do a five-minute warm-up. Legs should be the best option to start since it is the body part that drains you the most. I can push myself to do ten sets of everything and finish with killer cardio until I am unable to walk. Until I collapse. Until my mind and pure will keeps me going. That has to be an excellent way to start

I finish all the regular exercises. Squats, Deadlift, walking lunges, leg extensions, leg curls, etc. ten sets each. My legs can still do more. But it is gonna be even more painful than any other method I have used before. What is coming, I never tried after a heavy leg workout.

I embrace myself mentally for what is to come. And I decide to wear the gravity suit they invented. I have no idea about the technology they use, but I know it is incredible. The suit itself doesn't weigh anything at all. Maybe less than a pound.

I have no idea what fabric they used; it's nothing I have ever seen in my entire life. It's a one-piece, black, with a menu on the bottom left sleeve to adjust the weight. The menu is not a screen. It seems to be uniquely integrated into the suit's fabric. Gloves and black running shoes are part of the suit; however, I don't think the technology extends to them.

I start putting the suit on. A zipper on the front, and you easily fit in. It also stretches as necessary. This is incredible.

I start by setting the gravity to times-two. I think I should be able to handle that weight spread on my entire body. As soon as the weight adds, it pulls me down. I am on my knees and hands. Jesus! I did not expect to have such a battle with this weight. I won't back down. I will get up and move. I pull all my strength, and with a lot of struggle, sweating like never in my life, I stand. As I try to walk, my head starts to hurt. My legs shake, and my body just starts to crumble. I hit the floor hard.

I wake up, but I am not in the facility anymore.

What happened?

The atmosphere is serene. It is dark but looks as if a historic bright full moon is illuminating the place. I am not sure if it is dawn or dusk.

At around one hundred meters, I can see a big pyramid. Is it Egyptian? No, that looks more like an Aztec pyramid. This looks a lot like…Tenochtitlan, an old city, now known as Mexico City.

There are two smaller pyramids to the left and right of the Great Pyramid. With a lot of trees and bushes that work as a perimeter to this beautiful valley. I give my first step forward, and the sky just lights up with millions of stars. Wow, I can also see nebulas, this is unreal. Breathtaking.

Jesus, just how hard did I hit the floor?

I keep walking, and as I get closer, I can see a wall moving on the Great Pyramid creating an entrance. It is dark, but my curiosity always gets the best of me. I decide to keep walking to it until I finally reach it. I look to my right and to my left, one gaze at the sky, big breath, and I walk in.

The path starts to illuminate. With every step I give, floating flames without its proper pine torch begin to appear. As I keep moving forward, I look back. It is dark. Just the flames in front of me keep burning.

I keep moving forward, and no more flames appear. I give some more steps, but no more flames burn. It is all dark.

Where am I?

All I see is darkness around me…wait, I see twinkles, lights starting to appear in the… ceiling…?

"Jako…Jako." I hear an echoing voice while I keep looking at what seems to be stars…more nebulas, like a tiny universe, forming in front of my eyes.

"Jako." The voice is becoming clearer, a deep voice that echoes all around me.

Where the hell am I?

"Jako!" The deep voice gets louder.

"Who the hell are you? and how do you know my name?"

"Jako, We know everything. That's the reason we are here. We know our Earth is being attacked, and we want to help. However, there is only so much we can do."

Who are you?"

Like a magical spell, wind and different colored glowing particles swirl and mix together to form a nine-foot-tall man with a very peculiar outfit that looks exceptionally familiar.

"God damn! You are gonna give me a heart attack. Why are you so tall? Why are you dressed like that? So…colorful?"

"We did not know you could be so humorous, Jako" Another giant man forms from ashes and wind behind me.

"The hell is going on here? I was training, and then I passed out. Oh, I get it. I am probably unconscious lying on the floor, and this is just a dream." I start to look around. "That's why I am standing in a dark room, with what it now seems to be lots of starts and faraway galaxies around me."

"No, Jako, this is not a dream. It is more like an Astral projection." A third being appears on my right side.

"God damn it. You really need to stop doing that. Are there any more of you?"

All three men are surrounding me. They are intimidating because of their physical composure. They are incredibly muscular. But they don't seem hostile. Their clothes, I know I have seen their clothes somewhere. They wear headdresses made from shells, metals, and feathers of all distinct colors. Each headdress has a different insignia designed on it. To cover their torso, they wear a 'tilma,' something that looks like a big blanket knotted over the right shoulder. Each of them is wearing a different color 'tilma,' green, blue, and golden. Right above the bicep and below the shoulder, they put a golden ring surrounding the arm to wear it as jewelry. To cover their bottom half, they had a "Taparrabo," a loincloth that is tied in the front. Right above their calves and around two inches below the knee, they wear some sort of accessory that hangs like a mini skirt for the calves—matching the color of their tilma. For their feet, they wear wooden sandals and also carry some sort of long walking stick with colorful feathers at the top of it.

"Jako, we are ancient Aztec Gods. I am the God of War, Huitzilopochtli. To my right is Tlaloc, the God of Water and to my left, Quetzalcoatl, the God of life and wind."

"I knew you looked familiar. I remember studying in Mexico about Aztec culture. Let me tell you… you are more impressive in person than those wall drawings the Aztecs made of you."

"Jako…" Tlaloc says, "we know everything that has happened in the past twenty-four hours. We know about the extraterrestrial evolving you and you, gaining powers that were only seen once before."

"Yes, but I lost my powers. I have no idea how to get them back. I am not sure Liath, the alien that evolved me is alive. Damn it, I don't even know if my kids and wife are alive, and I am here talking to three tall, muscular colorful men in a dream. Wait…hold on a minute…" I cross my arms. "You said my powers were once seen before?"

"Yes. Liath, the Alien that 'evolved' you only unlock the potential you already had. That is why your change was so drastic. Do not worry, Jako; we know how you can get your powers back."

"Really? How? Tell me now!"

"How rude," Quetzalcoatl says.

"I am sorry I am just desperate. my family... humanity needs me. By the way, who had powers before?"

"During the fourteenth, fifteenth and sixteenth centuries when the Aztec people governed Central Mexico, they believed in three entities that reside in their bodies. Teyolia, Tonalli, and Ihiyotl. These three entities together brought health and longer life to humans. However, only one Aztec could attain such deep meditation to bring all of them together to achieve the full potential of these three entities. Malak, he evolved, he became the most powerful human to ever live. He had the power and knowledge of the ancient Aztec martial art, Yaomachtia. However, his mind was corrupted. Humans can be a dangerous species," Tlaloc explains.

Huitzilopochtli puts his right hand on my left shoulder. It feels so warm, and I feel so small, "Jako. This human who was so powerful was one of your ancestors. You are a direct Aztec descendant..."

"What...? Are you serious?" I gape. I am not sure what to feel. "How do you know this?"

"Because... We are Gods." Tlaloc's eyebrow rises.

I chuckle and say, "it makes sense."

"Jako. Therefore, we are here. Earth is in danger, and we cannot physically do anything about it. But you can. Earth's fate is in your hands. Only you can become this Aztec warrior, your ancestor once was. And of course, hopefully, you can control

144

such tremendous power and not become corrupted."

"But I am terrible at meditating. I can't, in a thousand years, make my head go blank. Besides, aren't there more Mexicans that are possible Aztec descendants?"

"No, Jako…you are the only true descendant. You are the last hope." Quetzalcoatl says.

Tlaloc explains, "Jako, to achieve the state of the Aztecs; you need to search for Teyolia, Tonalli, and Ihiyotl inside your body. It is a Quest."

"Ok… So, how do I do this?"

"The entity Teyolia is situated in the heart. Tonalli is located in the fontanel area, and last but not least, Ihiyotl: That can be found by the liver. You have to go in a deep trance, not just to empty your mind but to use your mind to go inside your body. You might achieve one of the three, or two at first. It is tough. That's why only one Aztec, during their entire existence, managed to get all three. It won't be until you get all three that you will gain full access to Aztec state and be as powerful as you can be."

"Jako, Jako, wake up." A familiar distorted female voice is heard loud, all over the dark space.

"Jako, Jako please come back."

I tilt my head up, looking around for the voice. The voice starts to clear, and I know it is my wife's voice. I bring my gaze down to talk to the ancient Gods, but they are gone. All the twinkling star-like lights start to shut off until the whole room I am in is dark.

I feel pain on my left cheek as a start coming back to reality.

Belisa's face is soaked in tears, and when I fully open my eyes, I can see her smile ear to ear. She goes down, as I am still laying on the floor, and hugs me. "Jako, I thought you were dead!"

I put my arms around her. "Belisa, everything is ok. I am still here."

"Jako, What happened? You never came back for us. You look normal again, did you lose your powers?

"There is a lot to explain. So many things happened these past hours. But I assure you I was taking care of you. They promised me to find you, all of you and bring you home. They are good people helping everybody. I don't know if you have met Miss Magna, but she is a good woman."

Belisa stops hugging me, and her tone of voice changes. "Oh Yes, I met her. A little bossy, I would say."

"She is alright," I reply.

"Jako, there is something significant you need to know."

"Would you first help me stand up, amor?"

Belisa stands up first and then extends her hand to pull me up. I still feel a little dizzy after the ancient Aztec ride I just had.

"First of all, are the kids, ok? Why aren't they here with you, B?"

"Yes, they are ok, Jako. I just thought I would get in here first by myself and make sure you were ok."

"I understand."

"Well Jako, this is gonna be disappointing –"

"- Liath is dead…?"

"How on earth would you know? Belisa says.

"Well, what else can be disappointing. Losing the kids or you would be a lot more than disappointing."

"I know Jako, but now that I see you with no powers, she isn't here to restore them."

"Well, I also have something to tell you that just happened to me while I was unconscious. However, I would like to see the kids first, then take a shower," I say and smile.

"I agree, you do need a shower," she says and we both laugh.

We hold hands and walk towards the exit of the room. The door opens, and the kids run to hug me. I can see some relief on the little ones and sadness on Logan. Logan waits for the little ones to have their moment.

As Luke and Minda come to hug me, I squat down to their height.

"Daddy, I am so happy to see you. I was so scared," Luke says.

"Yes, daddy, you never came back, and horrible things happened." Minda's voice starts to break.

I hug both of my kids with a firmer grip. "I am so sorry, Minda and Luke. I promise you I will never be away from you guys again. Ever again."

I call Logan with my right arm to join us in a big family hug, Belisa comes right after.

A few seconds pass, and I stand up.

I direct my attention to Logan. "Son, are you gonna be ok?"

Logan looks away, making a significant effort to hold his tears. "I will be Dad." Then he brings his sight back to me with his eyes emotionally compromised. "You taught me to be strong, and now is when we must show strength."

I walk towards my son, and I grab him and hug him. "Son, to be strong, is not to hold back tears. To be strong is to drop tears for those we love and fight for them. Even if they are not our race…Liath deserved better."

I move away from the hug and still holding his shoulder with my right hand. I say, "I will take a shower, and after that, we will sort this out, alright? We will survive. I have a plan."

Logan nods, affirming, and I walk away.

Nineteen

Teve - Jako

6:13 a.m.

Liath's death was unexpected. I really hoped she could've helped me get my strength back. However, there is no time to lament her death or overthink what she could have done. I must figure out the way to get to the Aztec state the ancient Gods told me about. I am still skeptical about what happened. I barely believe in the Christian God Belisa believes in. However, time is running out. Humankind is being slaughtered by the minute. At this rate, there will be no humankind to save. Also, it could be a matter of time before they find this secret facility. So, either I believe and try or don't do anything at all and die.

I finish taking the cold shower I always take. I have no idea how Belisa can shower at such elevated temperatures. I guess it's a woman thing.

I get dressed and walk towards the door, grab the knob, and twist. Lizi is there.

"Jesus…" My heart skips a beat.

"No… Just me," Lizi says and chuckles. "I am here to take you to your family, Sir.

"Lizi, what did we agree on?"

"Oh, I am so sorry, I just can't get used to it…Jako"

"Much better. People calling me 'Sir' makes me feel…old."

"But you are in your mid-thirties. That's not old at all."

"It is just something mental, I suppose," I say and laugh.

"Well, Jako, just follow me, and I will take you to your family. Let me see if I learned all the names. It is your wife, Belisa. And your kids, Luke, Minda, Logan, and Shum."

"Oh, no, no, Shum is just a kid we found a few hours ago."

"Oh, ok, do you know if he has any family alive?"

"I didn't get a chance to ask. I fought the aliens, and then you guys kidnapped me." I titter.

Lizi giggles awkwardly then says, "well, Jako, from what I hear, you didn't look so mmm human at the time."

"I guess."

How can I gain those powers back? I need to go back to that room and train. The best will be to have a nice breakfast with my family and forget a little about what is going on. And about two hours go back to my training.

"Jako…Jako…?" Lizi's tiny hand swings up and down in front of my face calling for my attention. "I lost you for a minute there. Are you ok?"

"I am ok, Lizi. Just planning out my day."

"Oh, you are one-off those that say, 'run your day before it runs you,' am I right?" Lizi says mockingly and chuckles.

"Yes, Lizi, I am just like that."

"Well, Jako, we are here." Lizi opens the door.

Minda and Luke are the first ones to run towards me and jump to hug me.

"Calm down kids, you just saw me a few moments ago." I smile.

"I know daddy, but we thought you were gone for good," Minda says with tears running down her face.

"Oh no, Minda. I'll be around for a while. We all will be around for a while. I am sorry I worried you guys." I direct my gaze to Belisa. "Amor, we need to talk." Then I turn to Logan. "Son, please grab the kids, I need to talk to your mother a few minutes."

"Of course, no problem, father."

Miss Magna is in the room, Lizi brought me to, and I ask her, "miss Magna, is there any room I can use to talk to my wife in private? I don't really feel like going back all the way to the room I slept at."

"Yes, of course, Jako. Follow me."

151

Belisa walks towards me and holds my hand. "Wow, this place is so nice. I wonder how much it cost to be built."

"I am not sure since I haven't really seen all of it."

As we follow Miss Magna, she says, "it cost 2 billion dollars to construct."

"What... you have to be kidding me! Belisa says.

"No, Mrs. Pineda, I am not kidding. I paid for it." She stops and turns. "Alright, this is the room. It's soundproof. And no Jako, it has no cameras. We can't hear you or see you there. So, talk freely."

"Right on, Thanks, Miss Magna."

Belisa and I walk in the room, and I close the door behind me. As soon as I turn, she jumps at me and kisses me.

We kiss passionately for a minute.

"Hey," I say while I caress her face with my fingertips.

"Hey," she sighs.

"I was so worried about you, Belisa."

"We were so worried about you too, Jako. We didn't know what happened to you, and we thought the worst."

Were you worried about me? I have...I had my powers; you and the kids were powerless."

"Tell me, Jako, what happened?"

"Well, B, I basically got kidnapped by Miss Magna's men. They thought I was one of them."

"How could they think that?"

"Well, it sorts of made sense. I looked different, remember?"

"You're right. Which brings the question, what happened to you? How did you lose your powers?"

In the room, there is a shiny, metal table and two chairs that are probably made of the same material. I grab Belisa's hand. "Let's sit down."

The chairs are across from each other like they would be in an interrogation room. Belisa grabs her chair and pulls it scratching the floor until she is next to me.

"I am not sure how I lost my powers. I got stung by a dart; then, I woke up in this bunker with no recollection of memories of how I lost my powers."

"Do you think maybe they did something to you?"

"I don't think so, amor. They are on our side. They wanna survive this too. If anything, they should be trying to replicate what I have or …had."

Belisa crosses her arms in front of her chest. "Yeah, that makes sense. Then what are we gonna do, Jako? We know these creatures are strong. Our weapons are not good enough. Miss Magna told me it took a very advanced rocket to bring down Liath, and they don't have enough. We need your powers."

I stand up, excited. "Well, Belisa, when I was training, I passed out. I was pushing myself so hard that I collapsed. I thought that could help to bring back my powers. Well, when I was unconscious, I had sort of a vision…"

"A vision?" Belisa stands up. "What kind of vision?"

"Well, I think I was visited by ancient Aztec Gods."

"Aztec Gods? But Jako, there is only one God. Those are ancient stories from Mexican ancestors. They are just like Thor or Loki from Germanic mythology."

"Be a little more open, Belisa. Look, I barely believe in God, and now I am asked to believe in a few." I chuckled. "that dream or vision. Whatever you wanna call it. It felt authentic. Like I was actually there with them."

"What did these 'Gods' say to you?"

"In summary, they said that I have an Aztec ancestor. So, Aztec blood runs through my veins. They know about Liath and what she did. They say that I could restore my powers by getting into what they called the Aztec State. But I woke up, and I have no idea what that means."

"How many people are in this place?" Belisa asks.

"I am not sure where you are going with this, Belisa?"

"Well, we can ask if anybody here knows anything about ancient Aztec history. Someone has to know...right?

"Maybe. We can try. Let's walk back and ask Miss Magna if she can ask on a microphone to the entire bunker if someone knows Ancient Aztec history."

I hold Belisa's right hand, but she lets go and hooks my left arm using her right hand to grab part of my bicep. We walk.

We get there, and the kids seem calmer. They have been through a lot; way too much in just a few hours. But they are strong kids.

"Father, is everything ok?" Logan asks.

"Yes, son. I am just looking for Miss Magna; I need her help."

"Well, she is not here. She told me to tell you that if you need her, she would be in the main room."

"That's perfect." Belisa, could you stay here with the kids. I am gonna run over there to ask Miss. Magna to announce the question so everybody can hear."

"Ok, Jako. We will be here waiting for you."

Luke gets close. "Dad. Don't take too long, please."

"I won't, son."

I run towards the Main room.

I really hope somebody here knows anything that can help me. Nobody else but me can save Earth. I have to do it.

I arrive to the main room.

"I am impressed," Miss Magna says without looking at me. "You can still run after killing yourself training. She turns around. "Your stamina is not normal." She raises her eyebrows amatively.

"Thank you, ...anyway. I need your help. Would you be able to ask something over a microphone, so everybody can hear and perhaps answer?"

"I am intrigued by Jako. What is the mystery all about?"

"I might have found a way to bring back my powers."

"Really? How?"

"There is no time to explain. The world is getting destroyed. Remember?

"I am sorry. You are utterly right. What is the question you would like me to ask?"

"I get closer to Miss Magna. Ask if anybody knows ancient Aztec History."

"Are you serious?" Miss Magna asks, skeptical.

"Yes, I am serious. Just do it."

"Ok, ok. Jesus."

Miss Magna gets close to a microphone. "Attention please, attention. This is Miss Magna. There is an important question I need to ask. Does anybody know…ancient Aztec History? If any of you know you would be of great help to our research on how to stop this invasion. If anybody knows, you know where to find me. I will be waiting. Thank you for your attention."

"Thank you, Miss Magna."

Miss Magna grabs a chair. "Now, we wait."

A few minutes later, someone shows up.

We see in the cameras a middle-age man, right outside the door.

"Lizi. Get the door." With a computer command, Lizi opens the door.

"Hello," the man says.

He is of average height. Somewhat overweight... He looks like a short version of a retired American football team.

"Hey." I walk towards the man. "How are you?"

"I am good. I heard your question over the speakers. They are ubiquitous." The man says with a peculiar British accent.

"Same with the cameras," Miss Magna says.

"Yeah… well, I am here to answer any questions you may have about ancient Aztecs. I studied a lot. In fact, I have plenty of knowledge of Mexican history."

"What are the odds? May I ask. Where are you from? I mean, don't take it wrong; but a white person knowing so much about Mexican history is something you see everyday. I don't even know

157

much about Mexican history, and I have Mexican descendants," I say and laugh.

"Jako. No time for that. Just ask the questions." Miss Magna gets me back on track.

"Yeah, alright. So-"

"Teve." Before I even ask his name, he cuts me off and says it.

"Teve. Do you know anything about Yaomachtia and the three entities?"

"Do you mean about Teyolia, Tonally, and Ihiytl?"

"Yes, Yes. That's it."

"Well. That is the science fiction part of the history of the Aztecs."

"What if I told you that it is real, and I need your help to learn how to get into the Aztec state and Learn Yaomachtia?"

"I would say that you, Sir, had me at 'it is real.' I will share all my knowledge. One question, though. How do you know about it?"

"Long story short, because... no time..." I give a quick gaze at Miss Magna. "...I had a dream while I was unconscious, and Aztec Gods told me about Yaomachtia and that I could achieve Aztec state because I was a direct descendant of the only Aztec Guy that did it back in the day."

"Cool." With his eyes wide," Teve says.

Miss Magna turns around. "Men."

"Alright, Teve. I am gonna take you to the training room, and there you'll teach me and probably train me on how to get the Aztec state." I wave my hand while walking away. "Bye, Miss Magna, and Thank you."

"Don't mention it, Jako. We all are here for the same cause. Just hurry, many soldiers and civilians are dying."

Twenty

Tonalli - Jako

7:43 a.m.

"Here, we are Teve."

"Wow, this place is amazing!" Teve's eyes wander around, stupefied.

"Teve, you haven't seen the coolest part yet. But tell me what I should do first? I am eager to start training!"

"I am sorry, I didn't catch your name, Sir," Teve says, still admiring the place.

I offer to shake hands. "I am so sorry. How rude of me. My name is Jako."

Teve shakes my hand. "What a solid handshake. By any chance were you in the military?" he asks, still shaking my hand.

I pull my hand gently. "As a matter of fact, yes, indeed. I served for many years."

"I can tell…anyway, let's start. Shall we?" Teve says.

Teve walks around the room slowly, and I follow. "Well, Jako, the three entities that the Aztecs had a connection with are potent. Anyone attempting to get these entities under control would suffer from corruption in their minds: Their very thoughts and feelings. That is why in the stories, the Aztec, Malak, who was the only one to achieve this full state in connecting all three entities, went psychotic. Power of any kind corrupts people. My question to you is, how do you know you would not become corrupt after tasting such power?"

I stop, and he turns around. "I have already tasted this power. It wasn't through an Aztec ritual or training, but I had power. And it felt good. I did have the urge to kill, and my thoughts were fogged, but I wanted to hurt only those attacking Earth. I came to my senses and was able to listen to my wife. However, I should also consider training my mind. So, I don't risk us all by being corrupted with the overflowing power I could achieve."

"You are right, Jako. It doesn't matter who you are, how strong mentally or physically you are. Power is addictive, and once you have some, you will desire more."

"I understand Teve. You seem very knowledgeable. And I trust you even though we just met. You remind me of my father. You resemble him."

"Really? Your father must be a very handsome man."

161

"He was. Just look at me. It runs in the family."
We chuckle.

"Alright, enough talk. Ready to start training?"
Teve says.

I make a fist with the right hand. "Hell yeah!"

Teve seems like a good person and an even better teacher. His British accent makes him sound so smart. I wonder if he has a family. If he does, I hope they are safe.

"Alright, Jako," Teve starts his lesson, "the first entity that you will try to connect with is Tonalli. The Aztecs believed this entity was located in the hair and fontanel area of the head. And regarding hair, you have quite a lot. I don't know exactly how to connect you with these entities, but I know enough to theorize. The word Tonalli has the root "tona," which means to radiate. As an experiment to start the connection, I will ask you to sit down, cross your legs, and close your eyes-"

"What? Am I gonna meditate?"

"In a sense, yes. However, you will not struggle at emptying your mind but focus on filling it up with warm thoughts, thoughts that give you the fire to fight this invasion. And concentrate it in the fontanel area of the skull."

"So, there is no physical training?"

"Jako, not everything is physical strength. Besides, you already have that. Connecting yourself internally with these entities will amplify it."

"Wow, that actually makes sense," I murmur.

I follow Teve's orders and sit down. I cross my legs and close my eyes. I start looking for those memories I have of my precious family. They are the ones who motivate me every day to be a better person. Belisa, my faithful wife, Logan, my kind son with the biggest heart, Minda, that selfless little girl, and Luke, the little mischievous, adorable kid; I would give my all for them.

I start to feel hot, very hot, just like when Liath gave me power. I can feel it again running through my veins. Yes, I am actually doing it!

I can hear Teve's voice. "Jako, do not lose focus; there are changes in your hair. Your hair is changing color intermittently between black and white. I believe this is part of the process. Keep going!"

My hair? I wonder what changes are happening. I didn't really see myself before.

And right there, I feel a pinch in my entire body, the air around me pops with the sudden loss of heat, and the rush of power is gone. I open my eyes.

"Bloody hell, what happened?" Teve says.

"I lost focus. Stay quiet, please," I say.

Teve clears his throat. "Alright, let's try it again. At least we know we are on the right path. This time try to remember strong memories and hold on to them. Things in your life that made you the happiest."

Without a word, I close my eyes, and I start to dig deep. The things that made me so happy were

163

the road trips. I can see Belisa in the passenger seat singing along me. Before we even had the kids. Those times were so simple and full of life. We were visiting Grand Canyon, Mount Rushmore, and Niagara Falls to mention some of the road trips we've had.

I start to feel the power again. I wonder if it is this easy because I've felt this before, or because Aztec blood runs through my veins. It doesn't matter; I welcome this power, my cells remember. My body remembers I need to keep bringing memories.

Minda's arrival in this world, holding her tiny little body for the first time. What a feeling.

I start to feel pressure on my forehead, but this is no headache. Could this be?

I hear a mysterious woman's voice, clear but low say, "Jako…Jako…"

What is this voice inside my head?

"Jako. Open your eyes slowly." The voice says.

"Who is this?" I ask while I keep my eyes closed.

"Who is who?" Teve asks.

I start to open my eyes slowly, raise my hand halfway, and look at them. I am glowing green! These light particles. What is this?

Teve has the broadest look I have ever seen in my life. "My God, the legend is real. You are part of the line Aztec royalty; you are the descendant of Malak, The Tlatoani, The King of kings! Your green aura and your white hair say it all." Teve kneels.

"Wait, white hair? Do I look like an old man?" I say while I stand up.

"No, no, no, you look amazing! This look totally fits you."

"What are you doing, kneeling, Teve? Get up, please."

"Whatever you say, deity."

"Listen…I am not a deity. I am just a human that happens to be of Aztec descent that grants him some powers. So, just treat me like any other person, ok?"

Teve gets up. "Ok, whatever you desire. But bloody hell. You look ace."

"Teve, I keep hearing a voice in my head. Calling my name. What is it.?"

Teve responds, "according to the legend, the entities are exactly that. They live inside you as a separate soul. They become part of you. However, they remain independent. You could lose them if you don't keep a strong connection."

"Yeah, but I did not hear that voice before. Why is that?"

"How did you get your powers before?" Teve asks.

"Well, Liath, one of the good aliens, had the ability to advance a species. And she did a ritual to 'evolve' me into what humans would look at the peak of our evolution."

"Wow, that's amazing. But perhaps, she only accessed the power you already had hidden within

165

you and brought it out without the connection needed to the entities, and that's why you lost your powers!" Teve says.

"This is crazy," I say while looking at my hands. "I can't believe I had this power inside of me all along. Maybe that is why I could always train so much for so long in one session, besting all of my fellow soldiers in the Black Jaguars."

"Now that you have successfully connected with Tonalli, let's see what you can do." Teve smiles, and his eyes widen even more.

"But what about the other two entities?" I ask.

"Jako, baby steps. You should control Tonalli one hundred percent before you overreach. Remember what happened to Malak when he got all power. He was corrupted."

"Alright! Alright. Understood. Time for me to show you the technology in this amazing training room. You are going to love it."

Teve puts his right arm across his stomach and rests his left elbow on it, while his hand grabs his chin. "The first thing I would like to test is your strength."

"Well, let me show you this state-of-the-art suit. It lets you add weight evenly throughout your body and stretches to any size."

"Put it on. I am tired of seeing you shirtless after your transformation ripped off your shirt."

I laugh.

I put on the suit and set the weight to five hundred pounds. The weight is nothing to me. I

166

keep adding, and I reach five tons. I still can move like I have regular clothes on.

Teve looks impressed. "Bollocks, that can't be right. How much more can you add?"

"I am not sure, let me press this —"

I am pulled down by the weight of fifty tons. I drop to my knees and can barely stand. "Jesus, I can hold fifty tons."

"Come, Jako, stand up; you got this!" Teve pushes me.

I struggle, but I start to stand. My forehead is dripping so much sweat. I finally stand up, breathing hard.

"We can safely say that your max is fifty tons for now," Teve says.

I look at him in doubt. "For now?"

"Yes, Jako, your power will increase once you get the other two entities under control."

This power is unbelievable. But is it enough? Last time that alien name Klatoth kicked my ass. But I hadn't accessed these Aztec entities before, voluntarily. Perhaps it gave me a boost enough to fight back.

"Jako, we need to keep testing your strength, speed, and other abilities that you may possess." Teve insists.

"I turn around. "No, this power should be enough to send those aliens back to where they came from."

"Jako, you are not thinking straight. That's the power talking. Think for yourself. You know that you ignore what you can do, and although you have powers, you won't be able to win if you ignore your abilities. Stop being careless. Please let's discover what you are capable of."

Teve is right. This power urges me to fight. My mind is stronger than this entity and its power.

I turned back to Teve. "Alright, Teve, let's train."

Twenty-One

Unexpected Visit - Belisa

10:43 a.m.

One of the qualities that made me fall in love with Jako is his big heart. He can be egocentric, sometimes a little arrogant, and even selfish (mostly with his time), but his big heart is incomparable. He loves it so much. He has a love for everybody, even for his enemies. However, his personality changed a little when he gained this power. I hope that he always remembers who he is.

My kids and I huddle together while waiting for Jako.

Miss Magna arrives. "Hello Belisa, may I call you Belisa?"

"Yes, that is fine. What is your first name?" I ask.

"Miss Magana will suffice," she says while crossing her arms in front of her chest. She seems a little uptight. Wearing a suit and high heels in this kind of situation seems impractical. "Would you and your kids like to see your husband training? He was successful in bringing his powers back, although this time, he seems a little different."

"Different? How?" I ask.

"Wouldn't you prefer to see for yourself?"

I turned around, and the kids are ready to go.

"Yes, Thank you."

Luke pulls at my clothing. "Mom, is my daddy gonna fight those monsters again?"

I try to be subtle. "Luke, your dad, is training to become even stronger, so if he fights those monsters, he will win. So, don't worry if he fights them again, ok?"

This doesn't calm Luke, but he remains quiet. I wonder what kind of thoughts ferments on my kid's head.

Shum is sitting on a silver bench that makes up part of the monotonous look of this place. "Shum, would you like to come with us?" I ask.

"As fun as that sounds…no, I'll stay. I think I might even take a nap right here," Shum says while lying down on the bench. "We got up way too early." He closes his eyes.

"Alright, suit yourself." I turn to the kids. "Are you ready to see your father training?"

"Yeah, mom, let's go!" Luke says.

We arrive at the training room, and I see him. A Green aura? But it used to be white? What is the difference now that he has recovered his powers? Perhaps the method through the Aztec entities made for a different color in aura.

"Wow, my dad looks amazing! And that black suit fits him well. He gains so much muscle when he transforms!" Logan says, impressed.

"I hope that he can beat those monsters. I don't wanna die just yet," Minda says.

"Don't worry, Minda. I know my dad can win. Just look at him." Luke points at Jako.

"All of you, don't—" A tremor interrupts me.

"What the hell was that? Miss Magna says. She grabs her ear, pressing her microphone. "Somebody tell me what that was?"

If Miss Magna is afraid, she can hide it pretty well.

Over the speakers, a panicked male voice yells, "This is a code red! This is not a drill! We are being attacked! A breach has been made; everyone trained for this take your positions now!"

"Miss Magna, what is going on?" Logan asks.

"Seems like the aliens have found us, and the facility was not strong enough," Miss Magna replies.

"Hurry, open the door, and let Jako know!" I order. "Seems like he didn't even notice the tremor."

"Alright, alright."

Miss Magna puts her hand on the screen beside the door, and it opens.

I crane my head through the open door and yell, "Jako, Jako, we are being attacked! The aliens have found us!"

Lights all over the facility start to flicker red. There is a loud, annoying alarm going off. This is happening for real.

Jako gets to us. "Are you serious? They are here?"

"Yes, Jako! they are inside!" Miss. Magna confirms.

"How do you know that?" Jako asks.

"Because, Jako, they just killed some of my men in the first line of defense upstairs, close to the surface."

"Alright, don't panic. I am stronger than the first time I had these powers. It seems like the ancient Aztec Gods were not a simple dream," Jako says. his lips form a sly smile. "I won't let anyone hurt you. Trust me."

Jako's aura grows more radiant. With flame-like tendrils of energy rising and disappearing into the air, like solar flares.

"Miss Magna takes my family to the safest room, the strongest you have. I will fight, and I assure you I will protect everyone with my life," Jako says.

I get in front of Jako and make the sign of the cross on him. "I know you don't believe in my God, but I do believe in him. He will protect you. Please be careful, my love." I kiss him like it is the last kiss I would give him."

"Come on, Belisa; we need to go!" Miss Magna urges me.

Jako goes back inside the room to take the black suit off and changes to his blue jeans that now barely fit his muscular physique. After he is done changing, he gets close to us and says, "Belisa...kids, I will win this fight. You are my biggest strength. I love you." Jako leaves with a green aura trailing him. He moves so fast he disappears in front of my eyes.

Twenty-Two

Second Encounter - Jako

11:03 a.m.

My training got interrupted by the desperate voice of my wife. We are being attacked by the aliens, and I am running towards the chaos above. I am unsure if I am strong enough to defeat Klatoth. The last time we met, he defeated me with ease. That bastard is strong. I'll do my best to win the fight and send them to hell. I won't let them hurt my family or anyone else.

The lights on the hallways change from bright white to flickering red. The alarm, like any other, pierces my cochlea. It is always annoying.

I start running. I am running so fast the people around me look paused.

I can sense a presence. How is this possible? Is this another ability of my new-found Aztec heritage power? I can sense three powerful beings. But one is more powerful than the other two. Could it be Klatoth?

They are on the first floor coming from the surface. I can sense them closer now. I guess I will find out who they are soon enough. As I use the emergency stairs to go up, I can't stop thinking about them, my family. They are my strength and my weakness. They are keeping my focus, strengthening my connection to Tonalli.

I stop and look around to see so many people dead already. They will pay for this.

"Sir... Are you the guy we brought in yesterday? The one with powers-?" A fallen soldier says while grabbing me by the ankle and spits blood.

I take a knee. "Yes, son..." He looks in his early twenties. "...I am the one you guys kidnaped, thinking I was one of them. But trust me, I am on your side. Tell me, who did this?"

The soldier is in agony, spitting more blood. "There were two monsters looking-creatures... and a girl."

A girl?... could it be...

"She announced herself as Aliza, daughter of King Danteloth." The Soldier coughs, whimpers, and in an agonizing voice, says, "please take my dog-tags and give them to my family. They should be in a safe room downstairs. Tell them I love them and I'm sorry I... I... could...not..."

The young soldier dies in my arms.

He confronted this threat, knowing he was going to die. This is bravery at its purest.

I yank his dog-tags from his neck and look at them. I'm so tired of this; people dying around me, my whole life. This needs to stop. Soldier Dastibas, I promise you; your family will know of your sacrifice.

I rise and concentrate. I close my eyes and sense their exact location. I open my eyes. Aliza, I will kill you!

I plant my right foot on the floor and make a hole. I take a sprinters position.

I start running.

In less than a second, I find them. "Hey, you have done enough damage to my city, to these people, to my world. That ends right here."

Aliza and her company turn around. "I see those tags in your right hand. Could they be from that young soldier? He is one of the bravest humans I have encountered. His loyalty, his selfless nature is admirable," Aliza says.

"I will wipe that smirk off your face. I will make you feel every single life you have taken." I power up.

My aura gets hotter and brighter.

The aliens acting as bodyguards are behind Aliza. They are even bigger than Klatoth, but the size is not everything. I move. In an instant, I am behind them. I can see Aliza following my movements with her sight, but the other two are way too slow for my speed. I make a fist and throw a punch with my right hand to the alien on my left. He goes flying against the wall. I look over quickly, and the other alien is barely looking behind him. I throw a kick with my left leg, and he goes on the opposite wall. Both made indents on the metallic walls by my force. I am definitely stronger this time around.

I look over where Aliza was supposed to be, but she was away a few meters from me. She has speed.

"I will let you fight them first. If you succeed, I will be your next challenger," Aliza says.

"Are you sure you wanna see your allies is dead?"

"Ha, you got a lucky shot." One of the aliens says while he cleans blood from his mouth.

"Is that so?" I say.

"Quiet! insignificant human. I will not let you keep being an inconvenience for us. Prepare yourself to be turned into offal," The other alien says.

"Hey, snails, I am the one waiting on you." I stand in a kickboxing stance.

Both alien's brows puckered into a frown. They pat themselves to shake the dust off. "Kill him!" one yells.

They move, but I can see them as if they were moving in slow motion. I elude every single hit and kick they throw at me. I can avoid the punches and still see Aliza crossing her arms in disappointment. She knows this will not end well for these two ugly aliens.

I must end this fight as soon as I can. Klatoth is even stronger than Aliza, and I'll need as much energy as I can save.

Dodge, jab, dodge, cross. Time for my attack. I intend to finish this fight in one punch, so I put all my energy into the punches. An uppercut to the Alien on my right, Hook to the alien on my left. They both go flying against the walls, and they look battered. They won't get up this time.

Aliza claps. "Wow, I am more than impressed—a human with such power. You are no ordinary being. Tell me, Earthling, what is your name?" She crosses her arms.

"Does it really matter? You'll die in a few moments after our fight begins. You won't need to know my name."

"Insolent. If you think I shiver in fear after seeing your fight with these minions, you are mistaken. As a matter of fact, I am excited. No one on this planet is strong enough. Your kind is brittle. Your condescending thoughts and arrogance are cementing your inevitable demise." She uncrosses her arms and starts walking towards me.

Suddenly she is not on my sight. She vanishes. Where did she go? I scan the place, just moving my eyes quickly. I take a defensive stance. Where the Hel —"

"Here I am… snail," she emphasizes.

Aliza's voice made me feel as if cold lightning went from my brain to my feet.

I feel a powerful punch on my back, and my body goes crashing against the wall. The entire front of my body hits one of the metal doors and cave the surface in. But my body isn't damaged, it seems to be more resistant than before.

Still, Aliza's punch hurts. She is a warrior, a very well-trained warrior.

I turn around. "Well, well, well. It looks like it is going to take me a few more moments than I thought. May I ask you a question, though?"

Aliza smirks. "So, now you are in a talkative mood?"

"I am just curious, why are you attacking us instead of trying to coexist? Liath, your Queen, wanted to have a peaceful agreement."

"Hahaha, Liath? I killed her a few moments ago."

"So, that was you?" I frown and make a fist. "All she wanted was the best for both planets, and you just killed her."

"I had orders. My father is the commander of my army, and he knows what is best for us. Your race is inferior yet dangerous. You have much violence in your history. Your kind is not trustworthy."

"Not all humans are like that. Some, like me, just want peace. I am sure we could have coexisted on this planet."

"Enough! You, Earthlings, are deceiving, I am here on a mission, and I will not fail my father!" Aliza yells.

She charges against me.

She moves so fast I can barely block her punches. They are so heavy. Left, right, kick, Knee. She is impressive. Our fighting speeds are matched. I have to lure her away from this place. This is not safe for the people taking refuge here.

I block her cross with my left hand and throw a hook with my right on her left cheek, and she crashes against the wall. It gives a second to run outside.

I run and make my way out through a large metal blast door.

A couple of miles away, she catches up, "I know what you are doing, earthling," Aliza says.

"My name is Jako. Guardian of this planet."

"Ok, Jako. Ready to die?"

Aliza is very motivated, but I can feel that those thoughts are not hers. She has been brainwashed by her father. Perhaps I can get through her.

She charges again to fight me. I know I can be faster than her. I close my eyes and think of my most warm memories. My family is always part of them.

I open my eyes, and Aliza's right fist is six inches from my face. I raise my left hand and block it. Her eyes widen in surprise. She throws continuous punches, but none connect; I can see all her movements. The stronger my connection to Tonalli, the more powerful I get. I wonder if there is a limit to this entity.

Now I have the advantage. However, I don't want to kill her; she seems so young and confused.

Her human form is stunning. She has big dark brown eyes, long, black and sleek hair, voluptuous lips, and a curvaceous body at about five feet five inches tall. So beautiful, she distracts me.

I move fast away from her punches and flank her. I wrap my arms around her and lock her arms against her sides. She squirms, trying to break my armlock, but I subdued her.

"We are not a threat to you. We should be able to come to an agreement to live together. I assure you there is more good than evil on this planet. Sure, we have our bad history, but the ignorant and scared majority have been controlled by the greedy, powerful, and ill-intentioned minority. I know I can change that," I say, hopeful.

Aliza stops struggling. "How would you be able to change thousands of years of the same? Just because you have these powers?"

"I believe people will listen to me, and those who don't will be put away."

She puts her head down. I can sense she is perplexed, thinking about what to do. I get distracted for a second with these thoughts, and she goes all out, breaking my lock. She turns around. "Prepare, Jako. You have won this fight, but I will return with stronger Klithans now that I know where the rest of you are hiding." She flies away.

I watch her fly away. So cool. I really wish I could do that. Maybe I can.

Twenty-Three

Aliza's Quandary - Aliza

11:13 a.m.

I wonder how much time my planet has left before it perishes.

My father stayed behind to make sure everyone came through. I admire him. He just wants the survival of our race. However, after fighting and talking to this warrior, Jako, is it possible to coexist? My father is entirely against it. He fundamentally believes that humans will never change their nature. They are indeed a young race. My father is wholly convinced of the course of action he decided to take.

I am perplexed. What a quandary this is. I want my species to survive, but I am hesitant about our method after being here and seeing how these people sincerely beg for mercy and acknowledging that many may just want peace.

Why do the powerful few always win? Aren't the masses strong enough? It's possible they are simply not educated enough. Have they put so much emphasis on wealth that power is based on that?

As I fly away, the warm wind flows over my skin. I look back. That warrior is still there. He could have killed me, but he spared my life. I know for a fact he was superior in every way. He had more speed and strength, yet he chose to let me go. Even after I said, I would come back with more Klithans to kill the rest of them.

I turn my head forward and continue flying over a smoldering city. I hope my father made it back. I need to talk to him.

The entire city is scorched by fire. Ruined human bodies scatter the landscape. We are taking this too far. I am part of it, but it does not feel right.

All klithans are equipped with a super microchip when we are born. This technology allows us to communicate and store information. This is how we can learn language from other species in no time. This chip is located behind our right ear in the mastoid bone.

I press the indentation in the bone to communicate with the others. "This is Aliza, daughter of commander Danteloth. I am ordering every Klithan to stop whatever you are doing and meet me at location 44.8756° North, 93.2131° West. If you, father, are here on Planet Blue, I also need to talk to you." I press again against my skull and cut communication.

I fly as fast as I can to the location.

I see it from far away. The same location I came through to this planet, a military base. As I get closer, I start to descend. The pain that Jako provoked in me is bothering me. He is powerful.

I touch the ground and walk towards the main entrance. This place is a disaster.

I walk inside.

There are more Klithans walking in. Some in-front of me, some are bustling towards another crowd making a din. The only reason this could be is that my father is here.

I hustle towards the furor.

Yes, indeed, my father is causing all this commotion. The surviving Klithans love him, and his rousing speeches.

"Father!" I yell from the crowd, "father, I need a word with you." I jostle forward. I make a second attempt from a closer range and no answer. I make my way and make it to where he is levitating. I tug his cloth firmly. "Father, we need to talk."

My father descends, and his feet touch the ground. He turns around. "Darling, can't you see I am talking to our people."

"Father, what I have to say is important. Do you not care?"

My father's gaze illustrates annoyance and is disguised right away by understanding. "Of course, I care about my daughter."

"Everyone outside, now!" he commands.

There is some part of me that always felt disconnected from my father. And today, that feeling is intensified. Do I really know him?

Everyone files out, and we are alone.

"Well, daughter, tell me what is so important?"

I am not sure about telling him that I have found the rest of the survivors. "Liath is no longer a threat."

He gets close to me, and extending his arms, grabs my shoulders. "You finally rid us of her? His eyes widen.

"Yes, father, as you asked."

"Where is the proof?"

"You don't believe me, father?"

"Of course, I believe you. I just desire to see the traitors head," my father says.

"I am sorry. I had to throw it away. It became a bother," I reply.

"It doesn't matter. Now we can conquer this world in totality with no worries. Humans are frail creatures."

"Yes, father –"

"Commander Danteloth," Klatoth interrupts. Being the right hand of my father, he feels entitled.

"Greetings Klatoth. Have you cleared this city? my father asks.

"Almost commander. Is everyone else here?" The grin in his face is intolerable.

"Not everyone made it. It was too late, and our planet was consumed by our star. I had to flee." My father's head lowers.

"I understand, Commander. It could not be helped. However, there is no time for condolences. Humans are indeed weak, but there is one warrior capable enough to be considered a threat."

Oh no, has he fought-…?

"His name is Jako."

Oh no, Klatoth has already clashed with this warrior. Does he know where he is now?

"Really?" My father rests the elbow of his left arm on his right hand while rubbing his chin, adopting a thinker's pose. "Did you take care of him?"

"I did not."

"What!... Why?" My father's arms drop. "That is unacceptable. Any and all threats should be eliminated."

"Commander, please calm down. He did injure two of our soldiers. However, his power doesn't compare to yours or mine..." Klatoth looks at me. "…or even to your daughters."

It is safe to assume that Jako somehow got a power-up because he could have killed me if he wanted to.

"Aliza, did you see this warrior while you were out?" my father asks.

"No, father, I haven't seen him." I have no idea why I just denied this, but it is too late to go back now.

"If you encounter him, finish him." He turns to Klatoth. "This is an order for both of you."

"Yes, commander!" Klatoth and I respond.

"Well, Klatoth, let me tell you: I am very proud of my daughter. She took care of the nuisance, Liath."

Klatoth has a sly smile, "Did you really, Aliza?"

"Yes, I did!" I respond.

I have a feeling Klatoth knows something.

Klatoth struts towards me, "Well, I know for a fact that the warrior you and I fought had contact with Liath, that's how he gained his powers: through her."

"Really? Now that she is dead, he should be much more manageable" Why do I keep covering for him? We could go right now and finish every human hiding in that facility. Perhaps, I am returning the favor of letting me escape. I can't believe my actions.

"Well, I believe you will kill him if you come into contact. You are also very powerful, and besides, you are the commander's daughter." Klatoth backs off, but I can see in his eyes he is not convinced.

I have never liked Klatoth. I have always felt that he hungers for power to the point of obsession. However, my father sees him almost as a family. Perhaps, he does consider him family. He is blinded

187

to Klatoth's power and hypocrisy. But I can see through him.

"Well, thank you both for the pleasant news. Now you and Klatoth have a new assignment. Search for that superhuman and bring him to me. I will show humanity that there is no way they can win this. After we demolish their stronger soldier showing it worldwide, their hopes will be crushed."

And now, I am stuck with arrogant Klatoth.

Twenty-four

Back-Up Plan - Jako

11:43 a.m.

Aliza...

I hope her head clears, and she thinks for herself. I am confident I made an impact on her. However, in any case, we will need to evacuate.

I run back inside the facility. Doors are crumpled like a tin foil; walls are damaged beyond repair, the entire top floor is a mess.

I continue downstairs.

I reach the last floor. I close my eyes and try to sense my wife. There she is. I am coming mi amor.

I walk towards the direction that I sense Belisa's presence. I can't see any entries for any safe room. Where the hell are they?

Suddenly, I see an anomaly, like pixels appearing on space. I stop and look carefully. It seems like a digital projection of the alley covering a door behind. I keep walking; the pixels completely disappear and reach the door. I skim the door with my right hand. It feels like it could stand a lot of damage. The door makes a metallic popping noise and opens.

"Dad! Dad! Are you ok?" Luke runs towards me, Minda is trailing him. There are a lot of people in the room.

"Yes, I am ok, Luke. There is nothing to worry about." I open my arms for his predictable jump on me. Right after, Minda joins the huddle.

"Seems like you have managed to scare the intruders away," Miss Magna says as I put down Luke.

"Well, there are two dead aliens on the main floor, and the third one, named Aliza, managed to escape. Which means we need to evacuate because she threatened to come back with reinforcements."

"How can you be so calm? Are you sure those aliens are dead?" Miss Magna seems irritated.

I walk towards Belisa and wrap my arm around her. "Calm down; I am sure they are dead. I felt their skulls collapse beneath my fists before they were flattened against the walls."

Miss Magna sniffs.

"How many survivors do we have here?" I ask, looking over to Miss Magna.

Miss Magna turns her head back, looking over her shoulder. "We numbered five hundred in this facility. But after this attack…well…." Her gaze goes back to me. "…much less. We are not sure if there are more of these things around the city."

I unwrap my arms from my wife and walk towards Miss Magna. "I know you are a woman of control, planning, and preparation for any kind of situation. Please tell me I am right when I assume that you have something planned for this particular situation."

"Well, Jako, you're quite intuitive. Yes, I presumed a scenario like this could happen, so I created a secret facility even stronger than this one. However, it is a lot smaller."

"I knew it. That is great news!" I say.

"What a woman, you are basically saving humanity from extinction," Belisa says to Miss Magna.

"Hey, what about me? I am the one actually taking the punches," I say jokingly.

Belisa and the kids laugh. Sometimes I need some comedy to get my head away from reality. But this reality is persistent and won't go away anytime soon.

"Alright, Miss Magna, where do we go?" I ask.

"Technically, we won't go anywhere. I built the bunker a mile away from here. The other side of this room has a door to a tunnel. When everybody crosses the door, I will press a button on this pen to trigger hidden explosives in the walls, and the entire room will be destroyed, so there is no way they can guess we are here."

"Wow, you really think about everything," Logan says, impressed.

I raise my voice. "Alright, everybody, we need to move quickly. Get in line as fast as you can; we have no time!"

The crowd starts to line up.

"Jako, I am so happy you are okay." Belisa grabs my left arm. "You always make me worry."

Belisa's tender look moves me. I have no idea what I would do without her. She is my column, my stanchion; without her, everything I have achieved means nothing.

Miss Magna turns away with a covetous look in her eyes.

"I am sorry B. It's not my intention to worry you. I just wanna be strong enough to protect you and the kids. You guys are my everything. And I would die protecting you." I hug her emphatically, "I promise that we will make it through this."

Logan, Luke, and Minda join the hug.

"By the way, where is Shum?" I wonder.

"I thought you would never ask," Shum says from afar.

"Hey, you are a survivor, aren't you?" I say.

Belisa laughs.

"Come on, let's go! We need to go!" I invite Shum waving my arm.

We are the last ones to cross the door. After a safe distance, Miss Magna opens safety on the detonator pen and clicks. A muffled sound, like an explosion underwater, and small tremors follow the click. The tunnel is made with metal all around, just like a regular corridor full of bright light.

We walk half a mile, and everyone enters the new facility. As I enter, I realize that most of the survivors are civilians.

Miss. Magna walks towards me. "Jako, I will be going to the main room to activate this branch of the facility. Do you think you could give me a hand?"

"I would like to be with my family for a few moments if you don't mind." I grab Shum by the shoulders. "Perhaps Shum can be helpful."

She gives Shum a deprecating look. "Do I have any other option?"

"Where is Liz? she could help you," I say.

"I don't know, Jako. I haven't seen her since the attack." Miss Magna looks away and walks with a surly expression.

Teve appears out of nowhere. "Hey Jako, I was waiting for all the commotion to be over to come and talk to you.

I turn my head, and Miss Magna is gone along with Shum.

What was that all about?

"By any chance, do you know if there is any room for us to keep training?" Teve asks.

193

"Uh…I…I don't know Teve; this is all new to me. But would you mind giving me a few moments with my family? I will talk to you in a few minutes."

"Yes, of course. Pardon my impertinence." Teve taps his quads, turns around, and walks away.

I feel like I haven't spent so much time with my family, and it has only been a day since this started.

"Hey." I gaze at my whole family. "I know this has been hard. We have never dealt with anything like this. This is the most difficult situation we have been through. You guys are my strength. And I know you worry about me when I am out there fighting. So, you should know that I'll be ok. Trust me. With your presence in my heart and mind, nobody can stop me."

"Father, we know that you are more than capable of handling one, two, or even three of the aliens, but what if they all attack at the same time?" Logan asks.

"I have a plan," I respond.

"Will you keep training, Jako?" My wife holds the kids as she is ready to let me be.

"No, mi amor. I will not be training anymore, for now. I have no time. We need to be ready for what is next."

"Daddy, are you staying transformed forever?" Luke asks me.

I take a deep breath, suppress the energy within me, and I return to normal. "Does that answer your question, son?"

"Wow, that's so cool. I wish I could be like you!" Luke says, excited.

"Maybe someday you will be able to. After all, you are my son…" I turn my look to Logan. "You too, Logan. Someday after this is over, I will train you both."

Logan is wary about this. "But you know I am-"

"Alright, I am gonna talk to Teve. You guys, don't worry. I will take care of this." I cut Logan off before he reveals the truth. The kids might not be ready to know.

Twenty-Five

Betrayal - Aliza

2:13 p.m.

I am unsettled about the true intentions of Klatoth. My dad venerates him, and it is obvious. But I cannot abide him. He is an arrogant fool that only wants to fight the strongest warriors and humiliate them. On the surface, he evokes loyalty. He behaves very well with my father and my mother before she died. However, there was always something about him. Perhaps his mannerisms, or his eagerness to please. I have always had a bad feeling about him.

Jako...that human has affected me. After utterly obliterating his city with plans to take his world, he let me go. I can't wrap my head around that. He is either extremely stupid or hopelessly compassionate.

The more I talk to father, the more I realize he has not taken into consideration that there are exceptions in every race, even if those exceptions are the ruling class. As Jako remarked, not all humans are violent; many want just a peaceful life. If we are here with the intention of genocide and taking this world for us, then we are no better than what we think they are.

I abscond from my father as quickly as I can. I do not like the idea of working with Klatoth in this. I shuffle again through the crowd and make it outside.

"Aliza, I need to talk to you." Klatoth has the audacity to grab my arm.

"Let go before I eviscerate the arm from your body," I say while grabbing the knife on the right side of my waist.

"Wow, Princess, why the hostility?" he says, still holding my arm.

"You know I despise you. I said, let go!" I furrow my eyebrows in a frown even more.

Klatoth changes his smug expression to a wry grin. "I know you know more than you are admitting." He finally let go of my arm.

"Think whatever your combat-damaged brain desires." I walk away.

He follows. "Your father and I have a long history. We fought against many enemies— rebellions, criminals, aliens that tried to take our world. We go back way before you were born. He trusts me. I met your mother even before your father; I saved her on many occasions. This is one of the reasons I am your fathers' right hand." Klatoth Stops.

Why is he telling me this?

I stop and turn around.

He continuous, "I am not sure what I did to you to deserve such treatment. Just like your father, I want the best for our people. And I know you are hiding something. I hope that you are not having conflicting thoughts about this... Are you?"

"Of course not." I walk a few feet to put myself in front of him. In his monstrous form, he is very tall. I look up. "And if you must know, I can see through you. You may have my father fooled but not me. I am young, not stupid. What is it that you are hiding, I wonder?" I turn around and prepare to fly. "Now, let's go."

Klatoth is right; I do have second thoughts about all of this. Humans are not all bad. I do not need more proof than that warrior to conclude this. He represents the good in humans. This city is in ruins, but I can still do something to cease the violence.

From afar, this planet looked beautiful, but now it is a wasteland. The humans' once-great cities destroyed. If I just become a spectator, I will never forgive myself.

Forgive me, father, I cannot do this.

I need to get away from Klatoth, but how? He has been right behind me this whole time. I know any opportunity taken to flee from him would be futile.

What can I do?

"Hey, do you have any idea of where you are going?" Klatoth catches up to me.

"I am just doing reconnaissance; I have no idea where to look. If you have any ideas, please enlighten me," I say.

"As a matter of fact, I do have an idea. You see this?" He digs a gadget out of his packet. "I am pretty sure humans are advanced enough to build underground bunkers. This device…" he admires it "…was created by our Military Intelligence to find these places. It sure comes in handy."

My face gets a cold rush, and my heart skips a beat. Human survivors are in danger. Klatoth will find them and slaughter them all.

"Look, I see something," I say nervously, right before he presses the button on the device.

"Where?" Klatoth looks down.

"Follow me." I rush down toward a massive, scorched building, feeling the warm air left from the fires.

I land, and Klatoth touches down seconds after me.

"I do not see anything, Aliza." He walks forward, just passing in front of me. "Don't play games with me."

I feel a rush of blood in my body. It is the adrenaline needed to do what I just thought. This is the only option and my most significant opportunity. I focus all my energy in my right hand, I know I will need everything I have to knock Klatoth out cold, even if he is distracted.

I make a fist and hit him in the back of his head. He collapses, and the device drops a few feet away. My hand is in pain. He is ridiculously strong. Jako will not be able to defeat him, not without my help.

There is no going back. I have betrayed my father and my people now. However, what we are doing is undeniably wrong. I must find a way to make peace.

I walk towards the device and pick it up. I put it in my back pocket and fly away.

I am unsure of how much time I have before Klatoth wakes up from my blow. He will be enraged. My father will be disappointed to hear that his only child is not supporting him. But I am sure he will get over it. His missions have always been more important to him.

I arrive at the location where the facility is supposed to be, and from up here, it looks like something bombarded the place. It could not have been us. The rest of the Klithans are back, worshipping my father. What has happened? Is that warrior gone?

I descend and look around at the mess.

I retrieve the device from my pocket, hoping there are still survivors.

I press the screen, and it flashes on, reading the topography of the landscape and the spaces underneath. It makes a beeping announcing it has located something—a half-mile north from where I am standing.

They have moved.

I fly as fast as I can and get there in seconds. I look at the screen, and it is telling me I am right on top of the anomaly. I look around but cannot see any entrance. They must have destroyed the other bunker as a decoy and had a tunnel to this bunker. Clever humans. But there must be an entrance.

"Hello there, I didn't expect you back so soon."

I turn around, and the warrior with the white hair is right behind me.

Twenty-Six

Truce - Jako

1:53 p.m.

I feel Aliza's presence, just her, nobody else is around. That is strange. Could she find no reinforcements? Or could I have gotten through to her? I gotta go talk to her.

She is right on top of us. How does she know about this place? Miss Magna said it was the safest place, but Aliza managed to find it this quickly.

"Teve, I'll be back later." I leave to see Miss Magna.

I run as fast as I can in my natural state. I see my wife talking with the kids. "Belisa, do you know where Miss Magna is?" I ask calmly, not betraying my worry.

"Not exactly, but last time I saw her, she went that way." Belisa pointed to a corridor going west.

"Ok, thank you!" I take a deep breath and start jogging away.

"Hey Jako, is everything Ok?" She yells right after I start jogging.

I turn around and jog back to her, "Yes, nothing to worry about mi amor." I give her a kiss in the forehead while I hold her arms. "I'll be back." I turn around and start jogging once again to find the bunker's creator.

I hope that Aliza's mind changed after we talked. Because if she is here, and revealing our position, we are in big trouble. I run to the end of the corridor and turn right, which is the only way to go. A door a few feet away opens.

"Miss Magna, I am glad I found you!" I say as soon as I recognize her.

"What is wrong, Jako?" She asks with a hint of nervousness in her face.

"One of the aliens that attacked earlier is back; her name is Aliza."

"Oh, God! Is she by herself?" Miss Magna covers her mouth with her right hand.

"Don't worry; she hasn't found us yet...per-se."

"What exactly do you mean?"

"Well, she is here on top of us, but she doesn't know our position exactly."

"You need to go out there and intercept her, now!" Miss Magna says. Her eyes are demanding.

"That is what I intend to do. However, I have no idea where the exit is located." I put my hands on my hips.

"Come on in." I follow her into a nearby room.

The room she was in was full of computers that probably control this facility.

"Jako, I have to tell you something. We have lost communication with the entire world. We are on our own."

"What? Since when?" I stop walking.

"Almost since the attacks started."

"And you just tell me now?" I scowl.

"I didn't want to distract you from your training with this situation. I was trying to handle it. Besides, you already have so much to worry about. However, it is impossible to do anything. The aliens have put a perimeter around the entire city, which cut us off from any kind of contact. What I am trying to tell you, Jako, is that we are on our own. And we could be the only ones standing against this threat. Please be careful." Miss Magna gets close and, out of character, hugs me. "I know you can save us all. Believe in your power." She takes a step back. "Now. Do you see that door?" Miss Magna points at the only red door across the room. "That corridor leads to an elevator a half-mile from here. Go, and please… protect us."

I nod. "I will. Please cover for me. I don't want my family to know about this. I'll take care of it."

"I will. Now go!"

I close my eyes, connect with Tonalli, and transform with a flash of green light. I enter the corridor and rush to the elevator in the blink of an eye. After what seems like an hour, but must have been only a few minutes, A beep announces that I've arrived at the surface. The elevator's roof divides into two and opens, revealing the sky. A metal ladder drops down from above. I climb and, after taking a breath of fresh air, run to Aliza's position.

"Hello there, I didn't expect you back so soon," I say from behind her.

She turns around. "How did you find me?"

"I am not so sure about that myself, but I can sense people."

"What? Really? What—

"Let me stop you there. You must be trying to distract me, killing time for your allies to come and help you wipe out the rest of us." I make a fist with my right hand. "But if you must know, I am even stronger."

I draw in more power from Tonalli, increasing our connection. My aura grows, becoming more intense.

Aliza raises her arms to cover the gust of wind and grit that could damage her eyes. "Warrior stop, I am on your side!" She yells.

"How can I trust you after you murdered your own Queen?" I yell back.

"I know you have no reason to trust me. I was just trying to please my father. But I realized he does

205

not care about anything, not even about me. He never did." She puts down her hands and yells, "I can prove it to you!"

I calm my energy. "How can you prove it?" I furrow my brow.

"Do you see this?" She grabs a device from her clothing and shows it to me. "This is a device developed to find hidden structures underground. This is how I found you. Klatoth, possibly our strongest warrior, was using it to find you, and I waited for the right moment to knock him out."

"Why would you do that?"

"What my father did on my planet, and is now doing with your people, is not right. I cannot stand by and do nothing. He is my father, but I have my own heart and beliefs. I now desire to fight next to you against my father, because I believe it to be right."

"I believe you."

"Do you? How can you believe me so easily?... I thought this would be much more difficult."

"Remember, I told you I can sense people. I can also sense when someone, even an alien, is saying the truth."

"I will stand alongside you in battle, with all I have until this-ends, Jako. My father started this genocide, and I followed blindly, trusting that he had the best interests of our people in his mind. I helped him; it is my duty to mend this." Aliza makes a fist against her chest. Her words sound genuine.

I move closer, and we shake hands. She is so beautiful. "My family is understanding, but I can't say the same for the rest of the survivors. I am uncertain of how they would react to finding out that an alien is fighting with us now. I will tell them I just found you out here rambling. Stay in your human form."

She nods. "Ok, Jako."

"Ok, now follow me, try to keep up."

We get back to the elevator and descend. The front door of the elevator opens, and I run. Aliza follows.

We go through the red door.

Miss Magna is still in the room waiting for me. "Is she Aliza?" She crosses her arms.

"Yes, she is," I reply.

Aliza looks at me and raises one eyebrow in confusion. "You said... -"

"Yeah, I changed my mind. I can't lie to them. It is how we build trust. People will understand." I gaze at Miss Magna. "Right, Miss Magna?"

Our benefactor uncrosses her arms, "Yes, of course. Apparently, we already had one ally from your planet... But you knew that. So, why not? We trust Jako."

"Listen, my father is very powerful. Klatoth is just below him in terms of their ability. Jako will not be enough." Aliza looks at me. "I mean with all due respect, no offense."

"None taken."

"Do you have any plan against my people?" Aliza asks.

Miss Magna walks to a desk close to her and grabs a glass filled with water. "Not really, this facility was mainly built for geohazard events, not exactly for an alien invasion." She takes a sip of water. "Until now, we have just been trying to stay alive."

"So, Jako, is your only weapon against us?"

"Yes. Your race is entirely more advanced than ours. Your technology and even biology are unmatched. We can't defeat you. It took our most advanced weapon to kill Liath, and that is a prototype. We don't have them in mass production." Miss Magna glowers.

"Ok, we are on the same side here." I get in between Aliza and Miss Magna. "Aliza, you and I have to train together and become stronger. I know I can handle most of your people, and If Klatoth and your father are as strong as you say, we need to train as much as we can."

"Train? what can we do in a day or less?" Aliza asks, perplexed.

Twenty-Seven

Realization - Klatoth

4:53 p.m.

I open my eyes; the ground looks blurry, the scorched trees cracked and sideways.

Aliza… she struck me. My head is spinning.

Traitor.

I move my hands slowly towards my head and ground them at my chest to support my weight as I push myself up. I feel so heavy.

That child had the audacity to deceive me and, in doing so, betrayed her entire race. Her harebrained actions put our survival in jeopardy.

I stand up and survey the area. She is long gone.

I knew it. As I suspected, she knows this warrior.

Where is my locator? No point in looking, she is smart. She would not have left it with me. Damn it. Now I have to go back to Danteloth and deal with his intolerable temper. He will be enraged about Aliza. I will kill her as soon as I get the chance.

I walk.

Aliza is a strong young woman, but she must have put everything she had into that blow. I will not be able to fly for a time.

We have really made a mess of this city, and we do not even know the name. The body count is unimportant. I am proud of my victories. We are here to stay; it is only natural that we displace the original inhabitants. And I only have one more obstacle: Jako. Although I am not sure that he will be a problem, even if he took my advice and has trained to become stronger. Either way, I am on top.

I try to fly. I feel better and manage to stay floating despite the pain in my skull.

Time to gather the rest of my people, to wipe out the last humans in this city. Including their best warrior.

I return, slowly, to our last location. I look for Danteloth. "Have you seen the commander?" I ask a fellow Klithan.

"Yes. He is over there." He points to the backyard of the destroyed building.

I walk towards him.

"Sir, I have news to report, I say, looking at Danteloths back while I approach him.

"Aliza has betrayed us," he responds as he turns around.

"Yes, Sir. I am sorry I was deceived."

"There is nobody around, Klatoth. Drop the formality."

"Are you not surprised, my friend?"

"Perhaps, but not as much as I would have expected. I was never there for her, and when I was all I did was train her, discipline her for her mistakes during training. She has a heart; I knew she was too soft for a campaign such as this. We are not. We do what is necessary."

Yes, we do. And always have.

"Danteloth, your daughter will have the same treatment as any other Klithan in her position."

"I do not disagree, Klatoth. She became a proselyte. If she sides with the humans, then she will die just like humans."

Danteloth was broken. Yet he showed true leadership, saying nothing of his grief. His eyes expressed more than his words.

"It is time to end this. Gather all our citizens. I must talk to them."

"As you wish." I retreated.

Danteloth has always shown resilience. However, I have known him for a long time. I wonder how long he can keep bottling his emotions. Even though we were born different from humans, we still feel. We are similar in that way.

211

I communicate with the rest of us with the chip in our heads. They gather around Danteloth outside.

"Our planet is gone. I was one of the last forced to leave home before it was enveloped by the heat of our dying star. A star that once gave us life. Many of us have lost family and friends. Many were lost even before the journey to this planet. I had to do things to ensure our survival. Queen Liath and King Lioneth were not ready for such a task. I have lost along with you. My daughter does not believe in our cause and has betrayed us; she will be fighting against us alongside humans. She is to be treated as one of them. She is no Klithan and is no longer my daughter. My fellow Klithans, train today and rest well tonight. Humans are brittle. They stand no chance against us. Tomorrow we unleash our full might and take this world. To survive, to begin our new empire. Tomorrow, we'll be chanting in victory. Tomorrow, we take the city and prepare this world as our new home. Klithans forever!" Danteloths speech motivates them to the core.

Danteloth and I go a long way back. I have no memories without him.

We were not born the natural way. We were genetically engineered to be who we are. Many Klithans are born this way. We were formulated to serve the needs of our society and, in turn, our civilization as a whole. We did not have parents, truly, or close family. We grew up together, we trained together, and we were told what we were.

The facility in which we were raised, to describe its size, was colossal. The inside had

212

corridors that could enclose some smaller human structures, with large numbers on the walls next to each door marking a room. The building was created using the most durable metal in the universe, known as Candelanium, to my people. The walls had two bars of light running parallel to the floor about 8 feet high, with a 6-inch gap between them. Green marked the East wing, orange the West, blue for North, and magenta the Southern wing. The center of the base held a space of about 200 meters long by 150 meters wide. This was where we trained. The entire structure was surrounded by a 6-meter-high wall with motion sensors, cameras, and an electrified barrier to keep anyone from going out or in.

In that same place, we would meet Sultath, Danteloth's now-deceased wife. I met her first, and I loved her first. I was training by myself. I always trained before anyone arrived, and after everyone left. She came one day during one of these sessions, and it was love at first sight. But Danteloth had the silver tongue and more presence. I have always envied that of him.

Danteloth and I became good friends. I am uncertain of how I have grown to hate him. I despised seeing him with her, yet I respected his vision and his wisdom. Everything he sets his mind to he does it.

Today, I am Danteloth's right hand. He trusts me without question.

My resentment against Danteloth has never completely vanished from me. He has never known about my feeling for Sultath. He could never read physical behavior that well. He has always been clueless as to what others really think. He never knew the grief I felt for his own wife's death.

I see Aliza, and I see her mother. Their resemblance is preternatural. I am unsure I will be able to do my duty when the time comes, though I know she must pay for her treachery.

Tomorrow will be an exciting day. Jako is not strong enough to defeat me, nor could he ever be. I could sense that in him. However, I must be prepared for everything. Human history shows that they can be resourceful when backed into a corner. Adding Aliza into the equation brings even more unpredictability to our encounter. I will be ready for whatever comes.

Twenty-Eight

An Ancient Art - Jako

2:53 p.m.

We have one day to train and rest. That is not enough time for our bodies to adapt and recover. We need more time. Miss Magna, Aliza, and I have no idea what to do.

I walk away from Miss Magna, and Aliza follows.

"Hey, where are you going, Jako? Miss Magna questions.

"I am going to see if Teve has any ideas; he seems like a pretty smart guy," I say without looking back.

Aliza is one step behind me, and she catches up. "Who is Teve?"

"Teve is a dude that knows a lot about my ancestors. He knew how to unlock my potential.

Maybe he has an idea of how to train more efficiently."

Aliza stays quiet.

"You will train with me. You also need to become stronger," I say.

"Well, hopefully, this Earthling knows something that can help us."

I stop walking and grab Aliza's shoulder with my right hand, "Wait, Liath had the power to evolve species, do you?"

"I do not possess that ability Jako. All Klithans have different traits and skills. What Liath had, the genetic manipulation of others, was a thing of myth."

"Damn it. I thought that perhaps, if you had that power and use it on my son Logan, maybe he could train as well and help us."

"Liath had a skill that was unknown to most of us. Not many Klithans in the past have been born or created with that gift." Aliza starts walking. "Come, we need to get to Teve."

We arrive at the main area where I saw Belisa last. "Amor, have you seen Teve?"

"Yes, but it's been a while. He was here and left to walk around the bunker. Is everything ok? Who is she?" Belisa raises her right eyebrow and throws a jealous look at Aliza.

I rub the back of my neck. "Well, this is Aliza. She is a Klithan, just like Liath."

Logan takes a closer look. "Wait…" Logan's face contorts in a scowl, his face betraying his rage, "You…" He points at Aliza, slowly. "…You killed Liath. You took her head!" Logan turns his gaze towards me. "Father, did you know about this?!"

"Son, please calm down. She is on our side. She was confused and wanted to please her father."

"Confused?" All of Logan's blood is rushing to his face. "How can you trust one of them? Especially her!" Logan's voice quivers.

"She was only following the orders of someone she trusted. We trusted Liath, and I had a good feeling about her. My guts are telling me good things about Aliza too. What she did was unforgivable. However, she knows what she has done and wants to make amends. And she has realized that what her father, the guy commanding everything, is doing is wrong. She is willing to fight with us and die with us if it comes to that."

Aliza walks to Logan. "I see that you cared for one of us. Humans have the capability to feel empathy for anything. The emotion your race shows has never been seen before in my race. Please, forgive me, Logan. I swear to fight along with you. I will kill my demented father if necessary."

"Listen, alien, I don't trust you, but I have never mistrusted my father's judgment." Logan walks away, scowling.

"Son, –" I call to him.

"Let him be Jako." Belisa cuts me off. "I will talk to him. If you think this is a good idea, we

217

support you. We always have." Belisa grabs the kids and goes after Logan.

"I am sorry to cause a disturbance in your family, Jako."

"Did you really take her head?" I question.

Aliza looks away. "I did. I was desperate for my father's approval."

"Jesus lady, that's barbaric." I walk away. She follows behind.

God damn it, Teve, where are you?

We have been walking for a while now, just wasting time. Aliza still behind me. She must be feeling down. We don't need that right now.

"Hey, don't worry about the past. The important thing is that you want to repent and are now fighting for the right thing. For peace."

Aliza smiles and catches up.

"Thank you for your support Jako. It was you who- "

"Jako." Teve interrupts Aliza.

"Teve! We finally found you!"

"Well, come look at what I've just found!" Teve is beaming.

With the door already open, I walk into the room Teve discovered. "Wow, this looks like a smaller replica of the other training room."

"Indeed, it appears so!"

"Just what we need!" Aliza admires the room.

Teve grabs my left arm. "Give us a moment, please." He tells Aliza before walking us away. "Who is she? She is bloody gorgeous."

I squirm my arm out of his grasp. "Her name is Aliza. She is an alien in human form."

"Jesus, never mind." The thought fills him with loathing. "Why is she here? Is she manipulating you somehow?" Teve snaps his fingers in front of my face.

"Stop that!" I slap his hand away from my face. "She is here to help. That's all you need to know. We have a problem."

"What is going on?" Teve gets serious.

"The entire invading army, they will come soon. Later today or tomorrow. We don't know for sure when, but we need to train and get stronger. Any ideas?"

Teve gets into thinkers pose, "Mm… how about you try to meditate and find the Aztec Gods that you had contact with before. Perhaps they can help. There is nothing that we can do here to help you get stronger; maybe they have something. We are far from inventing a hyperbolic time chamber," Teve says and chuckles.

"I believe you are onto something."

"Do we have a plan?" Aliza asks from a few meters away.

I walk back and explain what is gonna happen.

"Ok, give me some breathing room." Aliza and Teve walk back a few steps.

I sit down and close my eyes.

My mind won't stop spinning though

I hear Teve mumbling. Aliza responds to him.

I open one eye. "Could you please shut up?" I close my eyes again.

Come on; I need your help.

I let go.

I have a strange sensation. My body starts to tingle, and abruptly, I feel my soul, or spirit, is being yanked from my body. The see my body still sitting there meditating, only for a moment. Suddenly my surroundings turn pitch black. I am floating in the middle of nothingness. Then I am at that ancient place with starry skies.

"Jako, you have returned to us," an echoed voice says.

"Well, humanity's last stand is… myself; And I don't have enough strength to fight back. The odds are against me. I thought you might have a few ideas on how I can become even stronger?" I look around.

"Ah…" One of the Gods appears in front of me, and I step back, stupefied.

"Why do you always have to do that?" My skin prickles.

"We know how to help you. But this will be intense, training with my companions and me. You will be here for what will feel like months."

"Months? Didn't you hear that I only have one day, and even that's a maybe?"

"This is our realm. Time here does not exist. We exist forever. While your spirit is here, the time on Earth is irrelevant," Huitzilopochtli says.

"Irrelevant? What do you mean?" I question.

"Time flows on Earth, but not here. When you get back, it will be like you were never gone."

"That is insane. Can I bring someone else to train?"

"You can as long as you trust them. Hold whoever's hand you will bring and ask them to close their eyes. We will do the rest. Go now."

I open my eyes.

"Shut up? We didn't say anything," Teve says.

"I already talked to the Aztecs. Aliza, come over here, sit down in front of me, and close your eyes. Think about nothing," I instruct.

"Ok," Aliza complies.

"Teve, wait here. We won't be gone for long." I wink at Teve. Aliza closes her eyes, and then I follow.

Our spirits are pulled into the Gods' realm.

"Aliza, we are here."

This time all three Gods are here. "Jako... and?"

"Her name is Aliza," I intercede.

"I can talk for myself, Jako." Aliza utters, "Hello, my name is Aliza. Nice to meet you." She directs her sight to the Gods.

"I didn't know you could be polite," I say and smirk.

"Shut up."

"Jako, we will teach you an ancient martial art, lost in time. You two will be the only ones with this knowledge."

"I can't wait for this! Who would believe that I would be training with Gods? I didn't even believe in Gods, and now here I am." I say to Aliza with a broad smile.

"Are they really Gods? My race always thought that it was a clever primitive idea to enslave people. Preying on the idea of never being alone."

"Don't you see them? Do they look normal to you? Look around; we are in another realm."

"It is hard to believe. My race does not believe in Gods. We are all Atheists," Aliza says.

"Are you finished?" Huitzilopochtli asks.

"Yes, yes." I raise an eyebrow to Aliza. "Stop asking questions.

"Wait, why can't you three just make me stronger without all of this need for training? You are all-powerful, right?"

Aliza gives me a look that says, "no questions, huh?"

"I will explain it to you in a way you will understand." Quetzalcoatl takes the place of his brother God. "Jako, your body must adapt on its own if you are to fully control your might. That is the way of humans, adaptation through struggle.

Many do not understand the pure potential of the human nervous system and genetic code, but just giving you the full force of your power would be overwhelming to your body and mind. You would shatter. That being said, you will stay in your normal state to train. Your body will become stronger with our training so that when you transform, your abilities will be amplified."

"Seriously? I have a concern, though. Aliza isn't human, though. If she hits me in my normal state, I will die instantly. She would crush me."

Huitzilopochtli approaches me. "Remember where you are, Jako. Nothing from your world applies here. You will be ok."

"Now…" Tlaloc, the God of water approaches, "…we will teach you Yaomachtia, the art we taught our people so long ago. Almost all the information about this Aztec Martial art did not survive the Spanish invasion. Most Mexican cities were burnt to the ground, along with all martial arts schools, codices, and scrolls containing the techniques of combat. However, we possess all this information. And we will transfer this knowledge to you."

Quetzalcoatl, the God of life and wind steps behind Aliza and I and puts his huge hands on top of our heads. "This is all there is to know about this deadly art."

I feel a warm, gentle thrust on top of my head, and my thoughts flash. He is done within seconds, and I feel memories where there were none before.

"You both have acquired knowledge no others possess. Now your training begins."

"But—" I am interrupted by an attack from Huitzilopochtli. What happens next surprises me:

I take down a God.

I see his great fist coming towards me, and my left-hand blocks him. With my open right, I hit the side of his neck. I use both hands to wrap his head in an inverse grip and use the weight of my entire body to spin his in the air. Before he falls completely, I grab his right arm and position my knee on top of his head as he hits the ground. While I use all my weight to crush into him, I keep hold of his left arm, ready to break it.

I let go.

"You are, indeed, a prodigy. Just as we suspected." Huitzilopochtli grins as he gets up.

"What just happened?" Aliza is astonished. "Those were formidable moves."

"That is Yaomachtia. It is a brutal martial art that focuses on neutralizing the adversary quickly and efficiently. The preservation of stamina is highly important in this martial art," Quetzalcoatl states.

We will train until you are unable to move. And you will rest as much as you need.

"I am ready." I look at Aliza. "Are you?"

"Jako, I was raised by Danteloth in a training facility such as this. I am more than ready. I am overqualified." She smirks.

"Now you are just bragging," I say and beam a smile.

"Let us begin." All three Gods say in unison.

"We will start this session with speed exercises. One of the most important things in battle is how quickly you can react and think to counter your opponent's attacks." Quetzalcoatl turns and points at a pyramid about two hundred meters away. "On top of that Pyramid, there is a golden eagle statue. Both of your weight will be slightly altered so that it is more difficult. Aliza, yours will be altered more so than Jako, since you are stronger."

The realm changes from darkness to being illuminated by a big, bright moon, the same as before; It looks so beautiful. You can see every star in the sky. It is breathtaking. The Gods glow and emit infinitesimal particles of light that disappear almost as soon as they appear—one after another replacing each other.

Quetzalcoatl moves his right hand like a magician, and my body suddenly weighs more than I can handle. "Damn, how many Kilos is this?" I struggle to get on my feet.

"Ah, this is heavy!" Aliza is also on her knees.

"Rise, I know both of your capabilities. Bring me that eagle!" Quetzalcoatl orders.

I struggle, but I get on my feet. I am sweating already. I look at Aliza. "I will win this race."

"I did not know it was a competition," She replies.

"It always is, my lady."

225

"My lady?" Aliza makes a bemused gesture.

I have unlimited time here to become stronger, but I will not rest. I will not give up; I will not give in. I will protect Earth even if that means losing my life in the end.

"Can you keep up?" Aliza starts to gain speed and creates distance between us.

"I won't let you get there first." I reach deep within for strength. My body is giving up, and I still have to climb the pyramid. The Gods are tough trainers. They are probably enjoying this.

Aliza is just a few steps in front of me. I reach the pyramid. Jesus, it's so high.

"Are you giving up?" She taunts.

"Hell no, I am amazed by all of this." I close my eyes, take a deep breath. Here I go!

I pass Aliza. "What-?" She can't believe it.

"I always save my energy for the hardest part. I always have reserves." I brag.

"Damn!" Aliza scowls.

I reach the top of the pyramid. The scenery from here is stunning. I could stay right here forever and be alright with it.

It takes a lot to raise my hand and grab one of the golden eagles. I feel so heavy. I sweat profusely, but I grab it and start descending. "See you when you get back, Snail," I tell Aliza, who is halfway to the top.

I arrive back, my body spent. "Here... you... go," I say, between breaths, dripping sweat.

"It took you long enough," Tlaloc says.

"Are you serious?"

"If we measure it by Earth's time, that was two hours," Quetzalcoatl claims.

"There is no way!"

It felt like days. I falter and fade.

Twenty-Nine

Training on a different realm- Aliza

Jako is an admirable warrior. Strong and noble… for a human. His will has no limits.

I get back minutes after him with my golden eagle. Jako is on the floor. "Is he ok?" I ask one of these beings. They may be powerful, and power must be respected, but I refuse to call them Gods.

"He will be fine. He needs only a few minutes of rest. He pushes his body beyond his limits, his basic human nature, and his true nature clash. That is who he is."

"May I ask you, respectfully, what are you really?"

"We were considered Gods by them and worshipped by them. And we nurtured and taught them. Your race could have been seen as Gods as well if you appeared to them in peace since you have knowledge and power much greater than the Earthlings."

"Are you saying that you are not-"

Jako coughing interrupts my conversation, and he starts to open his eyes. "What the hell happened?"

"You fainted," I say.

"Ah, I did not! I just needed a nap. Wow, this exercise really kicked my ass."

"This was only the warmup, be ready for a hand to hand combat against Aliza. You will have more eagles to grab later," one of the three beings say. Their names are too complicated to pronounce.

"Alright, get in positions. Use the knowledge transferred into your brains," another being directs.

"Are we gonna fight with this weight on us as well?" Jako asks.

"This increase in gravity will be your burden at all times," One of the deities says.

"Fight!" Another command.

Here I go.

It is impossible to run with these suits. It is like we are fighting in slow motion.

Jako tries to lift his arm high enough to punch my face. I struggle to lift mine as well to block him. I just evade it, and he loses balance.

"Jako, you have to be prepared for anything in battle. now get up and focus." One of the deities turns his eyesight to me. "Aliza, good job eluding that. Great thinking."

Jako gets up, "Again!"

"So competitive."

"I will wipe that smug look off your face." Jako grins.

We continue fighting for a few minutes; they drag on like hours.

"That is enough for today. Rest. Tomorrow will be a harder day. Consider this only the warmup," the beings say in unison and disappear.

I drop to the floor.

Jako follows seconds after, "this past 2 days have been just incredible."

"What do you mean?"

"Well, my planet gets invaded by your people. The queen of your plant gives me powers. I get kidnaped by my own people; then, I woke up tied to a metal table with no powers. I met some Aztec ancient gods that give me power. Met you, who beheaded Liath, and you betray your people after meeting me. And now we are training together with said Gods. I know I missed some stuff, but that's basically it."

"Wow, your last two days have been… busy."

"I am starving!" Jako says.

A table loaded with delicacies appears. Jako's face expresses intense joy. I had no idea humans could feel such love toward sustenance.

We get up and sit down by the table, ready to finish all the food.

"Wait, if we are just astral-projections of our bodies, and our physical bodies are not here, are we really eating?" I question.

Jako looks at me. "Who cares, I'll enjoy this food anyway. The Gods would say that it's good for my mind."

How can humans have this much optimism? His planet is being taken over, his people are dying, and he still does not crumble emotionally.

"Jako, can I ask you a question?" I speak with a mouthful. "How do you do it?"

"How do I do what?" Jako does not cease eating.

"How do you keep going? Your world is being destroyed; your people are dying, your family could also die."

Jako ceases eating. "Life is too short to worry about anything. You had better enjoy it because the next day promises nothing. I can't be worrying about what I can't control. I fight for the best outcome, and that's all I can really do every day. And that is exactly what I am doing right now. I am the support of my family, and I must be strong. I have to. The world needs my power, and I will use it for the good of all. As long as my family is safe, I will fight, so they stay that way."

Jako leaves me speechless.

I can say with conviction that I have made the right decision.

Jako, you are unbelievable.

We both return to eat delicious food on the table.

Thirty

Calm before the Storm - Jako

3:23 p.m.

Our training is over. I feel more ready than ever. I feel so much more durable. This Godly training really paid off. I am sure I can win. I am ready.

"Thank you so much, Huitzilopochtli, Tlaloc, and Quetzalcoatl. I am in your debt." I kneel. Aliza stays standing.

"You owe us nothing, Jako. It was a pleasure to train such a noble warrior. We wish you prosperity," Huitzilopochtli says.

I stand up and reach for Aliza's hand. "Let's go, Aliza."

She holds my hand and closes her eyes. I do the same.

"Back soon? You're both going somewhere. Wait… you seem different. Both of you," Teve says concerned.

I smile at Aliza. "We were in the realm of the Gods for almost six months." We start to get up at the same time.

"There is no way! How is that possible?" Teve asks.

"I have no idea Teve. They are Gods. They won't tell me all their tricks."

"Wow, this is bloody amazing. What did you learn?"

"Oh, Teve! I learned an ancient Aztec martial art!"

"Do you mean…Yaomachtia?

"Yes, Teve. A very effective martial art."

"Oh, mate, did you really? Bloody hell. Do you feel stronger?"

"Much, much stronger. I am ready to confront them. All of them. Aliza got way stronger as well."

Aliza steps up. "Not all Klithans are as strong as Klatoth, my father, and me. We can deal with them. Some have strange abilities, but not all are suitable for combat. Yaomachtia is a rare martial art that will give us the edge we need."

"So, what do we do know, Jako?" Teve asks

"We prepare, rest, and wait."

"Are you planning to take them out? just you two?" Teve asks.

"Yes, we won't put any more lives in danger. Now, if you don't mind, I will go talk to Miss Magna and then my family." I walk away, and notice Aliza is not following. I stop and tilt my head. "Aren't you coming?"

Aliza shakes her head. "No, Jako, I will stay here with Teve. You need time with your wife and kids.".

"I am coming with you, Jako." Teve hastens.

"Don't be scared, Teve. She won't eat you." I raise my hand as a signal to stop.

"B-B-But…" Teve's voice falters.

"Keep her company; I'll be back soon." I continue walking away.

What intense training I had. I never thought I could reach such high potential. It is insane. And to think that there is still more potential after I can control the other two entities.

"Dad, you are back! That was quick!" Luke yells from a few meters away.

"Hey!" I wave my hand.

Luke comes running.

"Hey, buddy, where is your mom?"

Luke points to the east wall. "She is over there, talking to my brother."

"Ok, I am gonna talk with them, ok? Stay here. By the way, where is your sister?"

"She is in the bathroom," Luke says.

"Ok, when she comes back, tell her to stay with you. I will be watching you guys."

"Ok, daddy. Good luck with Logan, he seems upset."

I smile and ruffle Luke's hair. "Everything is gonna be alright. Trust me." I walk towards where Belisa and Logan are sitting.

"Hi, son. How are you feeling."

Logan remains quiet and crestfallen with his elbows resting his arms on his legs.

Belisa stands up and whispers to my ear, "talk to him, I'll be with the kids."

I nod and see her walk towards our kids.

I sit down next to Logan on the cold metal bench attached to the wall. I embrace him with my left arm. "Son, I know how you feel right now. But we need to trust Aliza. She is on our side. She made mistakes just like we have. Remember, we were her enemy."

Logan raises his head. "She cut Liath's head from her body. How is that a mistake? She wanted to do it. I saw the hate in her face."

"Logan, she was following orders from his father. Her emotions were manipulated; he made her do it. She was trying to please him. She was only looking for her father's acceptance and her own pride."

Logan stands up with a frown and clenched fists. "I really hope you are right about this. Have you thought about her infiltrating us? What if she

235

betrays you and ends up killing mom? Or the kids or all of us when we trust her?"

I stand up and take hold of Logan's shoulders, "Of course, son, but you know what, I have a good feeling about this. We also need her help. I can't win this fight on my own."

"I just hope you are right." Logan yanks out of my grasp and walks away.

"Logan…Logan!" My yelling is in vain.

"Hey, Jako, I thought you were gonna be training," Miss Magna says from my side."

"Yes." I tilt my head. "I am all done training."

"What? It hasn't even been ten minutes since you left my office." Miss Magna puts her right hand on her hip.

"I trained in the realm of the Aztec Gods. Time in that realm doesn't pass. If I were to put it into perspective, I was gone for almost six months of training," I say.

"I am just getting used to all of this. And since we have aliens invading us, I will just accept it and move on. Do you have a plan?"

"The only plan that I have is to wait for them and fight them. Aliza and I will be the only ones out there. You will maintain calm in here while we confront them all."

"Humanity still has hope, and it is all thanks to you." Miss Magna hugs me.

I put my arms around her. "You are the one that gave us hope. Thank to this facility, humanity has a chance. I am gonna give my all to protect Earth. We will not perish. We will come out on top and rebuild what they have destroyed."

I hear somebody clear her throat. "Jako, what is going on here?" It is Belisa's voice.

I let go of Miss Magna and turn to Belisa, "Nothing amor! Miss Magna was just thanking me for fighting the invaders."

Belisa looks at Miss Magna with a defiant chin thrust. "I see."

I look over Belisa's shoulder, and I see Teve and Aliza coming towards us. "Hey, double-time, I need to talk to all of you." They came right on time. I hate awkward moments like this.

Belisa can be somewhat jealous. And Miss Magna is a very attractive, successful woman. This could not have gone very well if it wasn't for Teve and Aliza arriving at this precise moment.

"Hey, Teve, Aliza, what is going on?" I ask.

"I am sorry Jako, I could not wait there any longer. She freaks me out." Teve's voice squeaks and falters.

"Shut up!" Aliza says.

I interpose, "Anyway." I look around. Belisa, Teve, Aliza, Miss Magna, and I see Logan coming to us. "We will wait a few seconds for my son."

Everybody turns their heads.

"Son, are you ok?"

Logan crosses his arms. "I will trust Aliza, just like you trust her. I don't believe her, but I believe

237

you, and we need to be unified if we wanna survive."

Aliza looks at Logan and gives a reassuring nod.

"Now that we are all here. I will explain what is gonna happen next. Aliza and I will be taking guard one at a time, so we can both get rest. We trained restlessly, and we believe we can beat them. Miss Magna will oversee everybody, keeping everyone safe in here. It is her facility, so I expect her to know where everything is, every room, etcetera...."

"Trus,t me, I know this place like the back of my hand," Miss Magna reiterates.

"... don't be scared. We'll survive this. Now let's go and have some food, enjoy the rest of the day. We don't know for sure when they will attack. When the night starts to fall, pick a room, and try to sleep. I am almost certain they will be here by dawn."

Miss Magna goes to the control room and makes an announcement for the survivors. Teve goes to find himself a room. I nod Aliza as a signal to let me talk to Belisa and Logan. She steps back a few feet.

"Both of you are pillars. I am who I am because of you. Thank you so much for the trust and support, but most of all, the love you have given me. Logan, you have grown into such a great young man. It doesn't matter that we don't share the same blood, you and I are so alike. Belisa, my wife, you

are my rock. I love you so much. Never forget that."
I hug them both, and they hug me back.

The worst is yet to come, but we will not back down.

Thirty-One

Third Encounter - Logan

Day 3, 3:03 a.m.

Two days ago, around three in the morning, my dad woke me up with a slap on my face. The city was being attacked. We didn't know what it was until we found Liath, an alien that tried to prevent a human genocide.

Two days after, here I am again, awake at 3 a.m. feeling so impotent.

Is there really nothing I can do to help?

If only I was a little more like my father. If I started training as he has for more than a decade, Liath could've helped me achieve my potential. I regret not listening to him and lying in bed most of the time.

Now my father is outside standing as our only hope, allying with Aliza, an alien we aren't one hundred percent sure we can trust.

I can't take it anymore. I can't sleep. I am so worried about this. My body starts to tremble like a tremor hitting the city and bringing down a building, and I am the building. I have to keep it together. My father is out there, and I am the one my siblings look after when he is not around.

But I need to do something. My bed feels uncomfortable. My body feels hot, and the room is around sixty-five degrees. I feel my blood rushing to my muscles as a signal from my brain to move them. However, I have no idea about what or how I would be of any help. If anything, I would become a hindrance to my father. Like grandma used to say, "mas ayuda el que no estorba." This closely translates to "more help is offered from the one who doesn't hinder."

But even with all the contradicting feelings, I get up from my bed, put on my shoes, and head to the door. I may not have my adopted father's blood, but I was raised by him. I know I can do something.

I press the red button to the left of the door, which changes to green and opens the door silently and slowly. I crane my head and look to both sides, making sure nobody is around. Like a thief in the night, I stealthily walk on my tiptoes, I don't want my mother knowing I'll be outside with my father, in case he needs me for anything. I can't just stay here and do nothing. I know fear lurks under my surface, but I won't let it control me. My father says that fear is just an illusion made by the uncertainty of the future. And I refuse to live enslaved to a stupid delusion.

I manage to make my way outside. The moon is so bright I can see around me very clearly; no clouds are covering the sky, no artificial lights are overshadowing the stars. It looks like a dream outside.

To my right, Aliza sits on the ground dozing with her back against a tree.

To my left, my father is standing with his back facing me. His arms are hanging at his sides, and his head is monitoring the surroundings slowly, resembling a robot.

"I know you are there, son," my dad says, without looking back.

I walk towards him and stand next to him. "Was I that loud?"

"You've never been very quiet, Logan," my dad says, laughs, and turns his head to see if Aliza got woken up. She is still napping. My dad continues in little more than a murmur, "you used to wake up and come downstairs, plodding that the house trembled."

"Really? I never knew," I say and chortle. I take a breath. "Dad, I am here because I wanna help in any way I can."

"Son, this is not one of your video games. If you die, you won't respawn here. I won't forgive myself if something happens to you."

"I know it's not a video game. I know the risk, but I feel so useless. I won't be able to forgive myself if something happens to you." I put my head down.

My dad grabs my shoulder. "Hey. You are not useless. You must take care of your mother and siblings. They need you, Logan. And I need you to help me with that. You have no idea how much weight you take off my shoulders while you are with them." My dad puts his right hand under my jaw and lifts my head. "I trust you."

I never thought my dad felt that way about me. I always felt as if I had to prove myself every day to him. He never really expresses his feelings towards me. I just assume things. These last two days, he has said more than the entire rest of my life.

"Ok, Dad. I'll do my best to not let you down-"

"Oh no, they are here!" My dad's face depicts worry while he looks at the sky. He orders me, "Logan, go inside and make sure you protect your mother and siblings! It is too dangerous for you out here." Then he runs towards Liath while he starts to transform. His green aura shines, and his hair changes to white. "Aliza, wake up! They are here!" He yells while running.

I am still standing in the same place.

"Logan, go!" my dad screams. "Go, go now!"

I start to run towards the underground facility. It is tough to let my dad face an army of aliens.

Good luck, dad.

I make it to the underground elevator entrance, and as I turn around, the aliens are landing. The area has some trees still standing around, and I decide to run and hide behind one of them. I know my mom and siblings are safe down there. The fight is imminent. Maybe I can help.

Aliza and my dad are standing next to each other. My dad's aura stops glowing.

A few feet from my dad, the aliens land, and the rest make a perimeter around them. One looks like a complete monster. His form resembles a black demon with big horns, humanoid but monstrous. The other one, a step in front of him, has a human form. I bet that is Aliza's father.

"Aliza," the human-like alien says while ignoring my dad, "are you sure that you desire this? To betray your people?"

Aliza takes a step forward. "Yes. I am certain. You never cared for anyone but yourself. You do not even care for me. You used me. This was not the only way to save our people. You are a monster."

"How can you say that, ungracious hellion!" His human form begins to contort and shift. His clothing fades as he grows larger than any human. His head takes shape, and four horns appear like a crown, two on each side. His skin changes color to purple, and his body swells. His legs gain so much muscle I can see the striations from here. Spikes grow from his elbows and upper back. His eyes go completely white. He is now probably eight feet, as large or even larger as the other alien near him. He is huge. He looks powerful.

"Are you Danteloth?" My dad clenches his right hand into a fist.

Danteloth slowly turns his gaze to my dad. "Yes, indeed, and you must be that Earthling causing me inconveniences."

"Am I? You are the one invading my planet, killing my people, and destroying our cities. Talk about an inconvenience," my dad replies.

The other alien takes a few steps forward. "Jako-"

"Well, you remembered my name, Klatoth."

"How could I forget it? I hope you are stronger."

"Oh, you have no idea." My dad smirks. He is so confident.

Danteloth intervenes, "we are here to end your pain and eliminate the last survivors of this city so that we can move on to the next one. Since we are low in numbers compared to your race, we will take city by city, expanding our protective field gradually."

"The only way you will be able to do that is over my dead body," my dad says, while preparing a fighting pose, I have never seen before. He plants his left foot in front, pointing forward, and his right foot right behind, pointing perpendicularly outward. His left-hand folds into a fist and his arm extends in front of his chest while his right arm flexes behind his head with his hand open like a claw.

Is this what he learned wherever he was training?

"And over my cadaver, father!" Aliza gets into a fighting stance similar to my father's.

I hear a mechanism being activated. Oh no, that is the elevator. It is quiet for them to hear at that distance. But I gotta go intercept whoever is coming up. Damn it!

I run, and as soon as the elevator opens, I jump inside.

"Mom, what are you doing here?"

"What are YOU doing here? She answers.

"I came to see if my dad needs any help."

"Are you crazy, Logan? This is not a game. We can't help your father. We just can't."

"I know, mom, but as I said to him, I feel useless. But he told me I was in charge of making sure you and my siblings were safe."

"What is going on out there? You jumped in here in a hurry!" my mom asks.

"The aliens are here and are about to fight my dad and Aliza."

My mom's face pales. "All of them are here?"

"Yes, mom. It is gonna be a very unfair fight."

"Ok, mmm, you go back and stay with your siblings, they are sleeping now. Don't let them come close here. I need to be here in case anything goes wrong. I must be a messenger to run back and tell Miss Magna we need to put plan C in motion."

"Plan C?"

"Don't worry about it now; we need to act fast."

"No."

"What?"

"I said 'no,' mom. I am not gonna leave my dad or you alone. I can help.

"Your siblings need you, Logan!"

"They need all of us, and that's why we are here. They will be fine. They are down there safe. Plus, Minda is the fourth oldest in this family."

We both stay and watch the confrontation.

I guide my mom out of the elevator and scurry behind the same three I was hiding.

My father's aura is glowing. He is ready to fight.

"Earthling, I propose something," Danteloth says.

My dad doesn't relax. "What is that?"

"I came to the idea to have all Klithans attack you, including Klatoth and myself. However, I see you are a human with honor and some skills. Someone like yourself deserves respect simply for his bravery. Because of this, Klatoth and I will be fighting you and Aliza. If you perish, we will take over the world as intended. However, if we lose, we will be exposed to your laws."

Danteloth is underestimating my dad. He seems very sure he will win. He doesn't know my father at all.

"Fight me. However, you want."

"I believe we have an agreement." Danteloth smiles.

My dad returns to his pose, and his aura shines once more.

"Let's begin." My dad dashes against Danteloth at speed I can't follow.

I see Klatoth appear in front of Danteloth and wallops my dad with a haymaker that he goes flying against a tree. "You got this wrong, weakling; you are mine."

My dad gets up as he had only tripped.

"Wow, you impress me. That hit would have knocked you out before," Klatoth says.

Aliza takes a fighting stance. "I've been ready for this day."

"Do you despise me that much, daughter?" Danteloth asks.

"I do not. I've only longed to make you proud. But it was all for the wrong reasons. Rethinking everything, I think I always execrated you. You never felt love for any being. And this invasion is proof of that. Your will to kill me proves what I unconsciously felt before about you," Aliza replies.

"My only desire was for you to be my successor. That is the sole reason I was so hard on you. And look at you now! What a disgrace. Fighting me in your human form. You quisling." Danteloth clenches both hands into fists.

The other aliens surrounding Aliza, Danteloth, Klatoth and my father open up, to give them more space to fight.

My father moves close to Aliza. "Are you ready?"

"I have never been readier. I know diplomacy is not and won't ever be my father's strength." Aliza and my dad power-up, yelling. My father's green aura gets bigger and brighter; his eyes glow white.

Aliza has a shining purple aura as well. Is this a result of their training?

They are done gathering energy and hurtle towards Danteloth and Klatoth.

My dad appears in front of Klatoth and Aliza in front of Danteloth. They exchange blows so fast I can only hear the sound of every punch. Every strike that is blocked produces a warm gust of wind that hits my body, like claps of thunder. Just how powerful are they? It's impressive to see. One of those hits would make me puree of tomato.

I turn around, and my mother has her right hand covering her mouth, watching the fight with distress.

Right behind her, an alien appears, and his fist pierces through her stomach from behind.

"MOTHER!" I yell. I look at my father as he turns his head over here.

Everyone pauses.

My dad yells my mother's name in anguish and rushes towards us. He flanks the alien, wraps his left hand around his neck and uses his right hand to tear off the alien's head.

My father is unrecognizable in his rage.

With one hand, he throws away the alien's body and with the other disposes of the head. Before my mom hits the floor, he catches her; tears run down his cheeks. He looks up and yells even louder, "NOOOOO!"

His body starts to let off steam; I can feel so much heat leaving my dad's body. His muscles show a river of veins, his hair and eyes glow even brighter, and unnatural green substance starts to appear over his skin.

Acknowledgments

I would like to thank, first, the very first person to know about this dream. A man who I owe so much and even helped to edit the grammar of some of the chapters of my first science fiction novel, my father, Steve Larsen. His wisdom, his teachings, and his words throughout all these years have been a treasure to me.

I would like to thank my mother who has, always and in a distinctive manner, tried to ground my feet. Mama Chave, thank you for keeping this dreamer, proud and egocentric person, somewhat humble.

I would like to thank my mentor Patricia Armstrong. Without her constructive criticism and without her belief in my writing, this book would, maybe, not had happened. Thank Patricia for believing in my writing and giving me the extra boost of confidence I needed.

I would like to thank a friend that has become so close to me in just a few months after meeting him. Jamison, thank you for your time. I know how we both are selfish with our time so that we can accomplish our goals. Therefore, I am in high debt with you; for giving me some of your time to help edit this book.

And last but not least, I would like to thank my beautiful wife, who has been supporting me for years— working along with my crazy schedule to make this dream happen, bearing my personality, my ego, and my pride.

Thank you! Father, Mother, and Beautiful Wife for being my wisdom, humility, and brace!

—

ANGEL SOLO

was born in Mazatlan, Sinaloa, Mexico. He resides now in Fargo, ND, where he writes, designs, works as a personal trainer and is a Sargent in the ARMY. *Jako The First Guardian: Book of Tonalli* is his debut novel in a planned trilogy. To learn more about Angel and his comic books series as well, visit aztekcomics.com